"FREEZE, YOU SON OF A BITCH!"

But the ragged-ass white man bulling Longarm's way didn't freeze. He raised the six-gun in his left hand, searching wildly for Longarm with his hat-brim-shaded eyes. Longarm fired low, folding the rascal at the belt line like a jackknife before he moved in, muttering, "It's about time I took one of the bastards alive!"

But despite being gut-shot the gunslick still seemed to have some fight in him. As Longarm bore down on him, he raised his Remington .44 again. . . .

TABOR EVANS

LONGARM

IN THE OSAGE STRIP

JOVE BOOKS, NEW YORK

LONGARM IN THE OSAGE STRIP

A Jove Book/published by arrangement with
the author

PRINTING HISTORY
Jove edition/September 1990

ISBN: 0-515-10401-9

PRINTED IN THE UNITED STATES OF AMERICA

10 9 8 7 6 5 4 3 2 1

Chapter 1

Longarm moved his prisoner from the back door of the county jail to the nearby railroad yards along about suppertime, when the light was sort of tricky and honest men were supposed to be more concerned with what was on their plates than they were with the comings and goings of federal felons.

But the bloody deeds Wee Willy Wiggins had been charged with had evoked a heap of attention as well as considerable loathing in this corner of the Colorado mining country. So it seemed he'd no sooner frog-marched the miserable little murderer aboard the narrow-gauge combination than the worried conductor joined him in the rear observation car to announce, "We got us a heap of grim-lipped mining men a-gathering out there in the gloaming, Deputy Long, and I doubt like hell they've showed up to ride this train down to Denver, hear?"

Longarm sighed, let the front of his tobacco-tweed frock coat hang open to expose the forward-facing grips of his cross-draw .44-40, and stepped out on the rear platform to discover that, however else they might be running this dinky mountain railroad, the conductor had been stating the simple truth.

The setting sun glowered through shifting plumes of sulfurous smelter smoke to cast hellfire beams of flickering illumination on the ever-growing crowd. With just about all of them yelling at once, nobody was making a lick of sense. Longarm drew his .44-40, which occasioned a moment of sullen silence. Longarm slid a sixth round into the chamber he usually kept empty lest he shoot himself or a friend in the foot without meaning to, and muttered to the conductor in the doorway right behind him, "Let me worry about these old boys whilst you worry about getting this infernal train out of here, *poco tiempo*!"

But the conductor muttered back, "They got a brewery dray across the tracks, up forward. I'd have never bothered you if there'd been any damned way to follow our damned old timetable."

Longarm swore softly and said, "Do the best you can up forward. Meanwhile I'll see if I can keep things civilized back here."

A self-appointed leader of the mob had overheard that last remark. So he shouted, "You can't, Marshal. This here vigilance committee means to treat Wee Willy as civilized as he treated that poor young gal he kidnapped and kilt!"

Another member of the mob, brandishing a two-by-four in one hand and a square can of coal oil in the other, chimed in with, "Damned A! Only we don't aim to rape the little shit. We just aim to burn his privates off afore we string him up!"

Longarm gripped the brass rail of the observation platform with his large free fist as he smiled down at their flickersome red faces, aware of how satanic he might look, right now, himself, as he raised his voice enough to be heard a ways back without sounding too sissy. He said, "You boys sound sincere but somewhat confused, no offense. To begin with, I'm not a marshal. I'm Deputy U.S. Marshal Custis Long, and I work for Marshal William Vail of the Denver District Court."

A sardonic-looking cuss, whose claw-hammer coat and flashy brocaded vest made one suspect him of gambling habits, called out, "We know all about you, Longarm. You don't know these boys all that well if you think you can stall for time till this combination pulls out."

A burlier man in need of a shave yelled, "This train ain't bound for nowheres afore you give us Wiggins and let us show him a thang or two about mistreating decent folk!"

The gambling man nodded and called out, "We don't want to hurt you or your fellow lawmen, Longarm. Just give us Wee Willy and you'll be free to go your own merry way. You know you've no call to risk a hair on your own head for that murdersome little bastard, if the truth be known."

A mining man with a rope of his own bawled out, "Give us that bitty shit if you don't aim to dangle at his side! For dangle he shall, afore this night be over, and I say anyone who'd raise a finger to help Wee Willy must be bad as he is!"

"Worse!" cried another voice from the crowd, adding, "We all know Wee Willy was ahint the door when the brains was passed out. A paid-up peace officer's supposed to respect and uphold the law!"

"And a woman's honor!" yelled the gambling man, brandishing a bitty nickel-plated H&R .32 Short as he continued. "That Indian agent's young wife had been dishonored all three ways afore Wee Willy finished her off, you know!"

Longarm grimaced and replied in a deeper, more intent-sounding tone. "Put that whore pistol away, tinhorn. As for what I know or don't know, unlike you gents, I've yet to hear evidence presented in court, either way. The prisoner my deputies are riding herd on, up forward, claims he had nothing to do with that kidnapping, let alone the murderous double cross it ended in. But you can all rest assured that since both the kidnapped lady and her late husband were employed by These United States up to the Shoshone Agency on the far side of the pass—"

"They'll get the slick-talking little rascal off!" another mob member cut in, adding, "Wee Willy was talking a

3

blue streak when the posse brung him in, and they say he had more than one rider half convinced by the time they got him into town! We want to make sure he pays for his devilsome doings, damn it! City slickers down to Denver ain't as likely to see through his innocent act!''

Longarm shrugged and called back, ''They'll hang him just as high as he deserves to hang, no matter what federal court hears his case. I hate to brag, boys. But I have to say it's a heap harder and surely more expensive to buy a federal judge and jury than your average homegrown variety.''

The gambling man, still brandishing that fool whore's pistol, called out, ''There's not going to be any trial in Denver for the little shit! What are we waiting for, boys? There's only one of him and there must be over a hundred of us!''

The mob swayed closer in with an ominous growl. One of them made the mistake of grabbing the brass rail, as if to haul himself aboard. Longarm knew the poor fool likely had a family to support. So he only broke the knuckle of the hero's left pinkie with his pistol's stocky steel barrel, and that seemed to do it.

As the unimportantly crippled miner fell back, clutching his hurt hand to his breast like a baby with the colic, Longarm called out, not unkindly, ''All right, friends and country boys, lend me your ears and listen sensible! For openers, this shit must cease! I can count as well as you boys can. So I know I can't stop all of you if you're all really serious about this. Now I want you to extend me the same courtesy and consider what I *can* do betwixt now and then. I got six in the wheel of this .44-40 and two more in my derringer. Saying I miss now and again—it's been known to happen— I still figure to take four or five of you with me, and naturally that figures to be the assholes out front. So, all bullshit aside, do any of you boys really aim to be out front when you can just as easily be in the back, like I always tried to be when the schoolmarm asked for blackboard volunteers to show the others some of that swell long division?''

4

There came a sort of sheepish collective chuckle from the crowd, and while nobody seemed to be moving that far back, he could see they seemed less intent on rushing him. So that was the way things had been for a million years. Then the conductor came back to announce, "The engine crew thought you'd like to know, Longarm: The sons of bitches up forward just ripped up a length of track. So even if we could shove our cowcatcher through that brewery dray, this train's not going nowheres at all tonight!"

Longarm growled, "You're a real bundle of cheer, ain't you?" as sharp-eared members of the mob relayed the ominous revelation in a jolly tone indeed. Longarm glanced at the western sky. The sun had almost vanished for the night behind the smoke-blurred black ridges over that way. It would soon be dark indeed. It was already getting tough to tell just what the murkier forms in the rear ranks of the crowd were really up to. As if to prove that great minds ran in the same channels, the dapperly dressed tinhorn eased closer, to call up to Longarm in a tone of sweet reason: "Give it up, amigo. There's no way you're about to keep this mob from having its way with Wee Willy Wiggins. So why take the risk of ropedancing by his side? Do you think the murderous shrimp would lift a finger to save you if the pants were covering the other ass?"

Longarm didn't answer. He shifted his six-gun to his left hand and got out a three-for-a-nickel cheroot as he continued to stare morosely at the setting sun. Another locomotive was chugging through the yards in the ruby light now. Some of the mob moved to make room for it. Nobody moved far enough to matter. Longarm lit his smoke as another voice in the crowd called out, "What are we waiting for?"

The gambling man called out, "Easy does it, boys. Never risk more than it takes to cover your bet! We know we got him. Give him time to *see* we got him. He wasn't whistling Dixie about them eight rounds at his disposal, you know."

"I want to burn off Wee Willy's cock and balls!" a less reasonable voice called out, adding, "I want to tear his haid off and shove it up his ass too. Then I mean to *kill* the bastard!''

Another member of the mob called out, less humorously, ''Shit, why not kill all of 'em. I don't know about you boys, but I say any lawman who sides with an outlaw is no better than an outlaw hisself!''

Way more than one other voice roared its full agreement to that last suggestion. The flashy dresser called up, ''You're running low on time as well as twilight, Marshal.''

To which Longarm could only answer, ''When you're right, you're right. But let me have a word with my own boys first. Billy Vail sent three of us to transport such a wicked little bastard and—''

''Make it snappy, then!'' The self-appointed mob leader cut in imperiously. So Longarm shot him a thoughtful look, nodded soberly, and ducked back inside the observation car. The one who'd expressed a desire to incinerate the prisoner's privates grinned wolfishly and said, ''We done it! We backed down the one and original Longarm! Let's git this over with, boys!''

But the tinhorn in the claw-hammer coat warned, ''Easy, boys. They say he's slick as banana skins on ice, and I for one would surely hate to die one minute ahead of Wee Willy Wiggins.''

He saw that he had their attention and added, ''We got 'em boxed good. Let's stay coolheaded and make certain none of *us* get hurt along with that outlaw we're after. Give old Longarm time to talk some sense into those other two deputies, the ones he calls Smiley and Dutch.''

The mob member with the busted knuckled grimaced and volunteered, ''I heard tell that tall breed called Smiley is quick on the draw as old Longarm hisself, whilst the stubbier one they calls Dutch is meaner than a wolverine with a toothache.''

The flashy dresser muttered, ''I just said that. I'd best mosey forward and make sure the boys at that end don't let anyone slip away in this sneaky light.''

Nobody argued. So a few minutes later the self-styled mob leader was free simply to swing himself aboard the platform of that other train's caboose as it slowly rolled past the stalled combination. He waited until they were chugging out of the yards onto the main, albeit narrow-gauged, line before he chuckled and stepped inside the dark interior of the caboose, saying, "That wasn't as tough as the boss figured it might be, after all."

Seated near the potbellied stove, cold at this time of the year, Longarm struck a match to shed some light on the subject. As the coal-oil lamp glowed warmly on all assembled in the cozy space, he grinned at the more elaborately costumed U.S. Deputy Guilfoyle to observe, "I always said a cuss who shaved so regular, and splashed so much bay rum on his fool hide after, had the makings of a born tinhorn, if not an outright pimp."

Deputy Guilfoyle joined in the laughter filling the caboose as he got rid of his fancy coat, vest, and whore's pistol. As he strapped his more workmanlike gun rig back on, he noticed the only one who didn't seem to find their recent playacting amusing was their small, drab prisoner, seated betwixt Smiley and Dutch and across from Longarm. Guilfoyle muttered, "He sure is a gloomy little shit, considering all the trouble we just went through to save him."

Longarm said, "Leave him be. Was I facing half the charges he's facing, once we turn him over to the tender mercies of that new federal prosecutor, my only consolation might be the simple fact that they can only use one rope per hanging."

Dutch nudged the handcuffed prisoner between him and Smiley to say, "Console yourself, you bitty rotten bucket of chickenshit."

Longarm blew smoke out both nostrils like a mildly annoyed old herd bull and repeated, "Leave him be. I mean it. The Constitution forbids cruel and unseemly punishment, Dutch."

But Dutch just looked back twice as annoyed and an-

7

swered, "Sheep-dip. There ain't no punishment I can think of that would fit the crimes of this here cocksucker!"

On the far side, Smiley said soberly, "Watch your mouth, Dutch. I know at least a dozen cocksuckers who've never sunk as low as this low-down . . . whatever. Try as I might, I just can't come up with a descriptive term for him as don't insult various bastards, sons of bitches, and such I've brought in in my time."

Longarm said, "Let's just call him a federal prisoner then, and let the judge and jury decide the exact terminology."

The little manacled man with the gray face and pale, pasty hair licked his ashen lips and murmured in a far-off ghostly voice, "I know none of you-all believe me, but I never done them bad things they say. I never even knew that gal married up with the Shoshone agent. So how could I have kidnapped her, done wicked things to her, and then bushwhacked her man when he rode out to meet me and my gang with all that ransom money? I never *had* no gang, durn it. I was riding all alone when they picked me up, and anyone can tell you I didn't have but three dollars and change on me when they did so. I don't know why they say I did all them mean things to them folk off the Indian agency. I never even met 'em. I wouldn't know 'em now, if they both come in to confront me this very minute!"

Dutch snorted and said, "Aw, for Pete's sake," and so Longarm, not wanting to deliver their prisoner all black and blue, said, "You'd best change places with me, Dutch. I'm more used to having 'em tell me how innocent they are and it's a long trip we got ahead of us."

Dutch rose, growling. "Suit yourself. But just for the record, have you ever yet had a sex fiend charged with two counts of murder tell you he was *guilty*?"

As they changed places their prisoner said, sobbing, "I ain't never in my life murdered nobody, damn it!"

Longarm sat down beside him with a sigh, saying, "Stuff a sock in it, Wiggins. We're not your judge and jury. We're

8

not even the arresting officers. Marshal Vail, in his infinite wisdom, just sent us to fetch you back to Denver, hear?''

Guilfoyle, who'd done much to assure they'd do so without as much bloodshed as Dutch or even Smiley might have settled for, hunkered with his back to the rear door as he opined, ''Longarm's right about it being a long trip, and like Dutch, I've yet to hear one of you shits own up to deserving the fate in store for you.''

''I paid for that little old mistake with that nester gal, cuss her tempting hide!'' their prisoner whimpered, adding, ''As to having raped the sass by force, agin' her will, I never! She never tolt me she was under the age of consent, and how was I to know they called that raping a statue? She warn't built like no statue, and she sure never moved like no statue in that hayloft. I swear she screwed like a natural woman, and whether she was really a statue or not, I served the ten damn years they throwed at me just for having my way with her that one time. Do I look dumb enough to go out and rape me another gal less'n six months after getting out of state prison after serving all that time as a statue rapist?''

Poker-faced, Smiley regarded Wiggins for a spell before he decided, ''You sure do. Our jobs would be twice as hard if you assholes all come up with new tricks ever' time they let you out, you know. The simple fact is that a lady was kidnapped and held for ransom, and then raped and murdered, along with her husband, after he'd paid the fool ransom.''

Guilfoyle growled, ''The more fool he, and the even bigger fool you, Wiggins. Couldn't you see that as the only man within a day's ride who'd ever done time for rape—''

''That's just it!'' their prisoner cut in, real tears streaming down his cheeks as he added, ''They didn't look for nobody else when they found that Indian agent dead and his poor wife dying. All she had to tell the sheriff was that she'd

9

been raped and shot by the same man as shot her husband. So guess who they rid right after!''

Longarm snubbed out his smoked-down cheroot as he told the little gray man, not unkindly, ''Save your story for the jury, old son. Even if you managed to convince us, we couldn't let you go at this late date.''

''Not even if you knowed who really done it?'' Wiggins asked him hopefully. Only to be asked if he had anyone who fit better than him in mind. When their prisoner confessed he had no idea at all who'd killed those folk and ridden off with that ransom, Longarm gently repeated, ''You're going to have to convince the jury, not us, and just betwixt the five of us, pard, you're surely going to have to come up with a better tale than any we've heard so far!''

Chapter 2

They had to change to a broad-gauge line about the time Longarm had planned on bedding that new barmaid at the Parthenon Saloon, and before they had Wee Willy Wiggins safely bedded down in their Denver lockup, even the Black Cat had shut down for a predawn mop-up and fresh sawdust sprinkle. Hence it was in a foul, as well as a sober, mood that Longarm strode into the federal building the next morning, only to be told by young Henry in the front office that for once he'd reported in too early.

Longarm cocked an eyebrow at the broad-ass daylight streaming through an eastern-facing window as he went for his pocket watch. But the dude who played their typewriter beat him to the draw by explaining, "The boss made as early an appointment as possible with his dentist. He couldn't find a dentist that opened before sunrise. I expect he'll be along anytime now. Is it safe to assume that federal want we sent you boys up to the Green River country to fetch would be over to the federal house of detention right now?"

Longarm nodded and said, "It would. I told old Billy when he told me to get up there that I didn't need three whole deputies backing me against a town that small."

Henry sniffed and said, "I'm sure you'd have brought

11

your man in, dead or alive, against all odds and all that guff. As I understood Marshal Vail's plan, the idea was to bring that rascal in alive, with as little damage as possible to his many admirers.''

Longarm chuckled dryly and replied, ''I reckon that vigilance committee is still trying to figure how we done it. Lord knows the poor little piss-ant never showed much imagination in escaping from anyone before.''

Then he glanced at the sunlight on the windowsill again and added, ''That reminds me of a promise I made him whilst half asleep aboard a night train. Tell old Billy I'll be back directly, and I'll be proud to sharpen pencils for you someday, Henry.''

Then he left before the clerk could ask just where he thought he was going. Longarm had learned way back in his army days that you got to go more places if you tried not to say just where you might be headed. He knew that had the boss been in, he'd have said not to pester other departments, even on the same floor, but a promise was a promise, even softly spoken while half asleep.

The female receptionist they'd hired for the new federal prosecutor seemed to know who Longarm was right off, even though he was sure he'd never ogled her seriously in the halls outside. For she was one of those perky little blue-eyed brunettes a man remembered once he'd ogled. She told Longarm to have a seat and scampered back to see if her boss would grant him the few minutes he'd requested.

Longarm remained standing, hat in hand, not because he felt all that humble but because it was commencing to hit him that he hadn't enjoyed any shut-eye for quite a spell. Like most men of action who kept themselves in fair shape, Longarm could stay awake and fairly alert for, say, seventy-two hours at a time, provided anything at all interesting was going on, but the saga of Wee Willy Wiggins sounded sort of tedious on the first telling, and Longarm was already having second thoughts about pestering the prosecution about a pretty open-and-shut case.

12

But the next thing he knew, the perky receptionist was leading him back to an oak-paneled office that seemed a sort of mirror image of old Billy Vail's, down the hall. Billy's banjo clock had been replaced by a framed Currier and Ives steamboat print, but after that the old architect who'd no doubt designed the whole building had gotten things about right. The dapper young squirt in charge of getting gents like Wee Willy hung was seated behind a desk that looked like the younger brother of old Billy's, and when he waved his cigar at a padded leather guest chair to Longarm's left, the tall deputy felt a mite like little Alice must have felt that time she stepped through the looking glass. He sat down, anyway, and, seeing that the other cuss was smoking, reached for one of his own cheaper smokes as the higher-ranking civil servant blew expensive Cuban fumes at him and asked what the hell he wanted, in as nice a way as he could manage.

Longarm got his own cheroot going before he pocketed the spent match, there being no damned ashtray handy, and said, "I got to spend more time with Wee Willy last night than I've spent with many a lady I thought prettier. Aside from the usual protestations of innocence, he raised some interesting points he might not have meant to. Few of us set out to impress the world as just plain dumb."

The sleek-looking prosecutor—his name was Clayburn, according to the even prettier receptionist—looked pained and replied, "If Wee Willy Wiggins is innocent, then we all owe an apology to Oliver Cromwell on the death of King Charles the First!"

Longarm shrugged and said, "I wouldn't know as much about *that* case. I've only been riding for justice six or eight years. It's true Wiggins has a prior rape charge on his yellow sheets, but there's still a heap of leeway betwixt statutory rape of a willing minor and downright dirty forcible rape. For openers, Wee Willy's barely big enough to overpower the average-sized female and—"

"Stop right there!" Clayburn cut in, putting his Havana

13

Claro aside to gather up a sheaf of carbon copies as he continued, glancing down at his notes from time to time. "The old chestnut charging the local law with simply rounding up local sex offenders until they could sort of force one into the glass slipper isn't going to work this time."

Longarm said, "Wiggins was the only newcomer to that county with such a record, you know. I, for one, find that sort of odd right off. Seems to me that you'd surely have at least a few more old boys with shady pasts in a rough-and-ready community that size and shape."

Clayburn snorted in disgust and flatly stated, "It wouldn't do your little friend a lick of good if you could prove the Marquis de Sade was in residence up yonder. We've got Wiggins dead to rights with a dying deposition. If the jury's out more than twenty minutes on this one, it'll mean at least one juror's deaf or dead drunk."

Longarm answered softly, "I'd be fibbing if I said I considered Wee Willy a friend, great or small, and I read our own onionskins of the arrest report."

But Clayburn must have wanted to refresh his own mind, for he insisted on repeating a lot Longarm already knew, beginning with, "Hamish Ferguson, in charge of the Yampa River Shoshone Agency, got back from a tribal meeting up on Elk Ridge to discover his wife, Emma, seemed nowhere to be found on or about the premises."

Longarm flicked ash on the rug as discreetly as he was able and cut in with "There's no argument about the ransom note he got a few days later, or the postmark on the envelope. Wherever they might have been holding Emma Ferguson, the mastermind posted his demands for all that *dinero* from the nearby county seat."

Clayburn dismissed him with a wave of his fancy cigar and bored on with "So much for that. Poor Ferguson withdrew the money to the dollar from his bank account. It was just about all he had after scrimping some on his modest salary. He did exactly as the ransom note demanded, save for one detail we now owe him a lot for."

Longarm nodded and said, "The kidnappers warned him not to say a word about their transaction to the law. But as he was fixing to ride out to meet 'em with all that *dinero* he fudged just a mite by telling the county law just enough to inspire some concern for his safe return."

Clayburn nodded grimly and said, "Exactly. Since Wiggins persists in his innocent act, we may never know all the details. But we still have more than enough to hang the son of a bitch! A deputy trailing Ferguson at a discreet distance heard the shots, spurred his own pony in pursuit, and arrived in time to find Hamish Ferguson dead on the trail, with his poor wife, Emma, dying less than ten yards farther along."

Longarm repressed a yawn and said, "Wee Willy must have really wiggled to come in her all three ways in the time he had to work with."

Clayburn shot him a disgusted look and said, "Don't be such an ass. The little monster had abused her, over and over, from the first day he'd kidnapped her at gunpoint. According to her own dying statement, Wiggins had made her ride to the ransom rendezvous with him, no doubt because her husband might not have handed the money over if he hadn't been lulled by her appearance, which was apparently safe and well."

"What was there preventing him from just gunning the Indian agent on sight and helping himself to the money?" asked Longarm lightly.

Clayburn shrugged and suggested, "Ask him, since you seem so interested in a shit-for-brains. Can't you see that pulling off a crime in a stupid manner doesn't constitute any defense at all? We don't need to tie up any loose strings that the idiot left dangling. The woman he'd kidnapped, abused, and shot down like a dog *identified* Wiggins as her tormentor! She died from internal bleeding, slow enough not only to name her killer but also to answer a few questions."

Longarm said, "Wiggins claims he never knew that Indian agent, let alone his wife."

To which Clayburn replied with a dry chuckle, "He claims he never *shot* either one of 'em, either. She said he did and why would anyone lie at such a time? Are you suggesting she was out to cover up for some *other* bastard who'd just raped and murdered her?"

Longarm sighed and said, "That do sound unlikely, don't it? I can see how a cuss trying to wriggle out of a killing would commence by claiming not to know a victim or more. A dying lady would be the better judge of just how well they'd been acquainted. To tell the truth, I'm more concerned about the brains behind the kidnapping than who might or might not have pulled any triggers. Having spent the better part of a whole night with the bitty rascal, I feel sure I'd have noticed if he'd shown any evidence at all of brains. He never did, and that sort of sticks in my craw, no matter how many times I try to swallow the indictment at face value."

Clayburn made an elaborate display of hauling out his fancy watch and checking the time as he replied, in a tone of dismissal, "Then it's a good thing you don't have to defend Wiggins in court. For whether you think he's guilty or pure as the driven snow, I'm going to demand the death penalty and *get* it!"

Longarm flicked more ash on the rug, not bothering to do so as sneakily this time, as he rose and replied, "I'm sure you take your job as serious as I take mine. I never come pestering you in hopes of getting Wee Willy off. I agree that a dying lady must have had a fair notion as to who might have murdered her. It's just that if we do hang Wee Willy high and sudden, we may never know who might have put him up to it. You say Hamish Ferguson got detailed instructions about the ransom for his wife, by mail. Is there any evidence Wee Willy Wiggins knows how to read and write? If there is, has anyone tried comparing the handwriting of that ransom note with his own?"

Clayburn shrugged and said, "No doubt the public defender appointed by the court will raise such questions,

Deputy Long. If you'd like to join the defense team, feel free to ask, but now, if you don't mind . . ."

Longarm put his hat back on with a grim little nod and allowed that he doubted his own boss would want him appearing as a witness for Wee Willy. As he left, he muttered for his own benefit, "I reckon half a loaf is better than none when you're fresh out of law school and out to build a rep, rapid. But I'd still rather round up one and all, and that poor little bastard's just too dumb, even if he struck us as vicious enough."

Out in the front office, the pretty little thing who sat about where ugly old Henry sat in Billy Vail's office dimpled sweetly up at him to ask if his interview with her boss had satisfied him and, if not, what else she might be able to do for him.

He doubted she meant that the way it could be taken, and in any case, it wasn't smart to mess with the gals where you ate or got paid regular. But rules were made to be broken in the interests of simple justice. So he smiled back at her just as wickedly and told her, "As a matter of fact, I'm interested in female intuition under pressure right now, and as you may have noticed, I'm not a female."

She looked away, her cheeks flushed temptingly, as she murmured, "The girls in the typing pool were talking about how masculine some of the gents working here in the federal building may or may not be, ah, Custis?"

He allowed that his dear old mother had been allowed to call him that without getting hit alongside the head, and she allowed that she wouldn't know just what those other gals might have meant, since she hadn't even been escorted home by anyone in Denver since she'd first arrived.

He said that seemed a mighty cold way to treat a new gal in town, and, one thing leading to another, the next thing they knew, they'd made a dinner date at Romano's and she'd said it was jake with her if he picked her up in here around quitting time.

17

He left her still flustered and strode back to his own office to see if he could get old Billy Vail to go along with a follow-up on those Ferguson killings. He knew that, not unlike himself, the crusty old marshal just hated to see big bad fish evade the net whilst overeager tyros were content to gather in the small fry.

But when he got there, Henry said the boss hadn't come back from the dentist yet. Longarm muttered something about fangs taking longer to fill than regular human teeth and allowed that seeing it was almost lunchtime, he might as well get started before other freeloaders got all the good stuff at the Parthenon.

Henry warned him he was likely to catch hell if he left that early. But Longarm pretended not to hear and, even so, just made it. For the Parthenon Saloon was famous for its fine free lunches and, sure enough, some son of a bitch had gotten into the pickled pigs' feet by the time he got there. Pickled pigs' feet tasted a heap better than they looked and were even more disgusting spattered with mustard and bread crumbs after some sloppy eater had been making sandwiches out of half of 'em. Longarm wrapped one pink trotter in rye bread and moved along the bar with a couple of boiled eggs in his other hand, to where Miss Trisha was pumping the suds with her own dainty paws. As their eyes met, she asked if he wanted the usual. When he said he was too tired for needled beer and just wanted suds, she shot a knowing look at the grub he'd helped himself to and murmured sweetly, ''Payday's that far off, huh? I was just fixing to mention a church social coming up this weekend too. But it'll be the day I wind up bidding on my own fool charity cake!''

Longarm knew he could still salvage the veiled invitation if he really wanted to, and he'd have wanted to if all they'd been talking about was the way she filled out that thin blouse and apron bodice. But as she slid the beer schooner across the wet mahogany at him, he just smiled sheepishly and said, ''It's impossible to hide one's sins from female in-

18

tuition, Miss Trisha. I played me some poker way past my bedtime last night. So I'm just about useless in more ways than one. I don't know how I'll ever make it through to quitting time, but I gotta."

She asked what time he got off, adding that she got off at six. He sighed wistfully and said, "I may be stuck later, as well as broke. Tell me something, as a female to a he-male, Miss Trisha. If I was to, say, show up here just after you'd been robbed and murdered, only you were still able to tell me what just happened . . ."

"Custis, is that supposed to be funny?" she cut in with a worried frown.

He told her soothingly, "I don't mean you, personal, exactly. I'm talking about another pretty lady who got treated mighty mean up in the mountains a few days ago. I wasn't there. I'm trying to picture myself in the place of another lawman who come upon her dying, see?"

Trisha looked relieved and said, "Oh, her. I heard some other boys from the federal building jawing about that Indian agent and his wife earlier today. You got the killer locked away good right now, though, right?"

Longarm nodded and replied, "We got him locked away, if she knew what she was saying as she lay dying. Speaking from your own experience as a woman, Miss Trisha, could you see yourself covering for a lover who'd just gut-shot you by accusing some other saddle bum entire?"

The ash-blond barmaid blinked in some confusion at him and replied, "Not hardly. Hell hath no fury like a woman gut-shot by a false-hearted lover. But I thought that rascal kidnapped her and, ah, forced her to be vile with him. Are you suggesting she might have really *liked* him—before he shot her, I mean?"

Longarm grimaced and said, "Not hardly. There's no accounting for tastes, but a halfway decent-looking woman has to draw the line somewhere and . . . Bless your smart soul if that's not something worth some serious second thoughts about!"

19

Trisha asked what she'd said that might have struck him as all that wise. So he explained. "When you hear a young wife's been kidnapped, treated just disgusting, and then killed, you tend to take it for granted she was pretty. But what if she was ugly as a mutt? Or at least ugly enough to fall for a plain, but not too grotesque, little cuss like Wee Willy Wiggins?"

Trisha shrugged and said, "My girlfried Gloria keeps company with a stockyard hand I wouldn't wipe my feet on, and she's not bad-looking at all. But what are we jawing about, Custis? Nobody's said that poor Ferguson woman run off with her killer, willing. He's charged with abducting her, then killing both her and her husband once the ransom was paid. So what difference could it make what anyone at all involved might have looked like?"

Longarm didn't want to talk dirty to a gal he'd never been in bed with yet, so he just stuffed his face a spell, and sure enough, she drifted off to serve other customers as the Parthenon began to get more crowded, both hands of the clock reaching for some sky.

Longarm polished off his pigs' feet and boiled eggs with head cheese and potato salad, washed down with the last of the lager, and headed back to the office, belching delicately until the short walk settled his somewhat over-seasoned meal.

As he rejoined old Henry in their second-story office the prissy clerk favored him with a now-you're-gonna-get-it look and informed him their boss was waiting in the back to hear his explanation for leaving that early for lunch. Longarm shrugged and muttered, "Shit, I've put in more duty time this morning on my hardworking legs than any old cuss could have in a dentist's chair."

"I heard that," rumbled Marshal William Vail from behind his desk as Longarm made it all the way through the door. Longarm didn't care. One of the reasons he and his boss got along so well was that unlike poor old Henry and even some of the other deputies, Longarm sassed the old

20

fart back. Billy Vail was one of those natural growlers who seldom really bit anyone who didn't have a good bite coming.

Vail was way shorter and fatter than Longarm, as well as a good deal older, and, Vail insisted, quicker on the draw. Since, knock wood, it seemed unlikely they'd ever meet in mortal combat, Vail expected Longarm to accept this as the word of a gentleman. Longarm took the stated age of a certain widow woman up on Sherman Avenue with a grain of salt as well, but being a gentleman himself, he never said so.

As he sat himself down near Billy Vail's cluttered desk, Longarm was glad he still had a couple of inches' worth of cheroot to puff on, for old Billy was stinking the place with one of those creations he kept mistaking for nickel cigars. Longarm had yet to decide whether they were rolled from skunk-cabbage leaves or worn-out rain slickers. They smelled a mite like both.

Blowing some plain old tobacco smoke back at his boss in self-defense, Longarm commenced to go into the Ferguson kidnapping and killings. Billy Vail hushed him and announced, "You ain't on that case. You never were, save as leader of the transportation team. Wee Willy Wiggins was never more than a sprig of poison oak as got nipped in the bud."

Longarm muttered, "Maybe so. There's still a few things as bother me about the official version of his various misdeeds, though."

Vail shrugged and told him, "If he beats the case in court, which hardly seems likely, I'll be pleased as punch to send you out after the sneaky little shit some more. Meanwhile, if it's all the same to you, this office has a caseload of shits we ain't locked up yet."

He rummaged through the snowbanks of paper strewn across his desk—Longarm vaguely recalled a green blotter somewhere under all that mess—and produced some printed forms that were clipped together. As he handed them across

21

to Longarm, he said, "You'll have to get off the Missouri Pacific along about Coffeyville, Kansas, and shove your McClellan, Winchester, and big ass aboard a livery mount from there on south. The department will spring two bits a day for the hire of the horse and six cents a mile for travel expenses. If you go charging any more bridal suites to your expense account, I swear it'll come out of your paycheck this time."

Longarm glanced at the printed form and cocked a thoughtful eyebrow. He'd seen this same sort of hunting license before. They all began, "A Warrant for the Arrest of————, certified to be a white man and not a member of any Indian Nation by birth or marriage or adoption into any Indian Nation, tribe, or clan."

Longarm neatly folded the sheaf of warrants and put them in an inside pocket of his frock coat, saying, "I hope you know what you and that judge just down the hall are doing, boss. I could likely flimflam the Indian police with a Chinese laundry ticket. But won't old Hanging Judge Parker over to Fort Smith offer to hang me if I go messing around in the Cherokee Strip with a warrant signed by the Denver District Court?"

Vail shook his bullet head and said, "No. Two reasons. I just got off a mighty polite telegram to Isaak Parker, and even if I hadn't, a federal want is a federal want. I doubt you'll wind up in the Cherokee Strip to begin with. The old gal we want you to track down and have a talk with was last noticed in about the Osage Strip, which is a mite far west for old Isaak Parker to police in the first place."

Longarm frowned and asked, "You're sending me to arrest a white woman dwelling in the Indian Nation, Billy?"

To which Vail replied, "Not exactly. If she hollers, you can let her go. The old gal's married up with a shady Indian trader suspected of running firewater to wards of the U.S. government as ain't supposed to drink such shit. But what we really want her to tell us about is her kissing kin, Frank and Jesse. You see, her maiden name was Younger, and

22

we now know the James, Younger, Miller, Ford and so forth Missouri tribes intertwine incestuously.''

Longarm stared incredulously and pleaded, "Jesus H. Christ, you can't send me to pester that old bawd Belle Starr again! Whether she had that bratty daughter by Cole Younger or not ain't for me to say, but the last time you sent me to Younger's Bend in the Nation and damn near got me killed, I did establish that neither Frank nor Jesse have been anywhere near there since the Northfield raid left their gang so crippled up.''

Vail blew a big blue smoke signal at him and said soothingly, "Pay attention to your elders and don't go jumping to conclusions, damn it. I just now told you I saw no need for you to go all the way east to the damn Cherokee Strip. This trader's wife is another gal entirely. Unlike old Belle Starr, she don't brag on screwing any of the Youngers. She *is* a Younger, making her some sort of kissing cousin to Frank and Jesse's dear old momma, Zerelda, and hence blood kin to the two most wanted owl-hoot riders on our shit list!''

Longarm rose to snuff his cheroot in a bitty clay sombrero on one corner of the desk as he replied, "I dunno, Billy. Some say Zerelda James Samuel is Cole Younger's favorite aunt, whilst others say the Jameses and the Youngers was no more than neighbors.''

Vail shrugged and said, "Whatever. The point is that Adeline Younger, the sister of the late Henry Washington Younger, is Cole Younger's aunt for sure and certain. Cole writes to her to this day from his prison cell, and guess who reads their mail?''

Longarm made a wry face, sat back down, and said he didn't have to guess. "If this white lady sneaking firewater to the Osage knows where Frank and Jesse have been hiding since that Northfield bank robbery blew up in their faces, why in thunder do I have to go all the way to the Osage Strip, damn it?''

Vail explained. "To find out, of course. Nobody in that

23

widespread criminal clan is about to put anything important down on paper. But mark my words, the only way we're ever going to round up the last of that gang will be with the help of their own kith and kin. The ones we have locked up keep bitching about being double-crossed by someone in Northfield. Not even the Pinkertons have been able to pick up a peep about the future plans of those still running loose. So it's safe to assume Frank and Jesse are not only lying low as a sidewinder's belly button but refusing to have anything to do with anyone they never giggled in church with in their boyhoods. They say Jesse's wife, Zee Mimms, is a first cousin and they were married up Methodist by their mutual uncle, the Reverend William James.''

Longarm chuckled dryly and said, ''I read about it in the social columns of the Kansas City *Dispatch* back in '74 or '75, under the heading about all the world loving a lover and the shotguns being trained away from the altar for a change. I hear Jesse and old Zee have at least two kids now. I wonder how many fingers, if not heads, the little tykes have betwixt 'em.''

He started to reach absently for a fresh cheroot, decided it was dumb to smoke such expensive ones when you didn't really have to, and said, ''I'd still rather work on something more solid than some old white-trash gal who might or might not have noticed Frank and Jesse at a family get-together one time. But I reckon you're right about 'em having more than enough to hang Wee Willy Wiggins. And if he has anything to say about masterminds who put him up to it, he'll talk as fast to old Clayburn as he might to me.''

He rose again, adding, ''I suspect I just missed the afternoon eastbound. But in case I didn't, am I just supposed to guess the name of this old bat you want me to scout up in the Osage Strip?''

Vail smiled sheepishly and handed him another typed

24

paper as he replied, "It's all here. Her married name is Dalton. Mrs. Lew Dalton. She and her whiskey-trading man have fifteen kids between 'em, all kissing kin to Frank and Jesse James, the dear little shits."

Chapter 3

It was funny, considering it had been old Billy and not him who'd spent the morning at the dentist's, but try as he might to put it out of his mind, Longarm kept running a mental tongue over those rough spots in the teeth of the case they had against Wee Willy. So seeing as he had plenty of time to kill if he meant to ride a certain night train free, Longarm moseyed down to the federal house of detention along about three that afternoon, to see if the poor little piss-ant wanted to change his story.

Wee Willy didn't. He kept insisting he'd had nothing to do with the crime, even after Longarm had lit a swell smoke for him. Longarm heard him out one more tedious time and then said, "Bullshit. I've been over the typed arrest report, Wiggins. It distinctly states Emma Ferguson accused you *by name,* not just a description you and any number of other saddle bums might fit. They're going to tie a stout plank to your back afore they drop you through the gallows trap, to make sure they bust your scrawny neck scientific, and when they do, you'll end up with the biggest hard-on you've ever had, only it won't do you or any lady you admire all that much good, of course."

Wee Willy said with a sob, "I know how cruel they mean to treat me. My mamma used to take me ever' time they held a public hanging in our town. Why are you rubbing my face in it ahead of time? I never done nothing mean to you, damn your big old mouth!''

Longarm said, "I'm trying to save you a sudden death with a hard-on and your pants full of crap. Anyone can see you never pulled off that crime all by yourself, old son.''

Wee Willy insisted, "I never done it at all, with or without a lick of help! The first I knowed about that Indian agent and his wife getting kilt by a person or persons unknown was when they come to arrest me, damn it! Why won't nobody believe me?''

Longarm grimaced and said, "For openers, Emma Ferguson never said she'd been murdered by a person or persons unknown. For another, the posse cut sign of at least one pony moving up and down that same fatal trail with mismatched shoes, just like the pony you'd tethered out front of that cathouse they caught you committing other crimes in. Fortunately for you, crimes against nature are taken more serious by the state of Colorado than the federal government. So if you'd like to set the record straight about just the raping of that kidnap victim . . .''

But Wee Willy wailed that he hadn't been doing half the things they said he had to that whore they caught him in bed with, so, seeing the truth simply didn't seem to be in the little shit this early in the proceedings, Longarm left him another cheroot and two matches, told him to think it over, and ambled out of the stinky cell block to enjoy some fresher air.

Fresh air was a relative term this close to the railroad yards, with the wind coming from the west. But coal smoke was still an improvement over the sour jail-house smells of mingled sweat and fear. Longarm strode absently east toward the federal building, until he wondered why in thunder he'd want to give Billy Vail another crack at putting him to work and, seeing that the day was about shot in any case, he just spun on the next boot heel as it hit the pavement and proved once again that the man who'd said virtue was

27

its own reward hadn't gotten out of the house all that much.

For although his intent had been simply to retrace his steps to a saloon door he'd just passed, Longarm found himself face-to-face at point-blank range with a pasty-faced youth wearing lots of black leather and a brace of six-guns. His pistols were still in their holsters. The sawed-off ten-gauge he was pointing at Longarm wasn't. It went off with a roar to rival the cannon out front of the State House up on Capitol Hill just as Longarm dived sideways through a plate-glass window for lack of anyplace else that looked even half as safe.

As he rolled over and over through busted glass and the ribbon bows of the notions shop he discovered himself in, he naturally got his own gun out and told the two ladies screaming at him like it was his fault to shut up and *duck,* for chrissake. By this time he was right side up again, albeit crouched low with the muzzle of his .44–40 trained back the way he'd just come. So when the bewildered back-shooter dropped his scattergun, drew his twin .45s, and moved in on the busted-out window, he naturally presented himself sideways to Longarm, as long as nobody worried about the glass door of the notions shop, as yet unmarred by so much as a crack.

Longarm cracked it good as he pumped three rounds, double-action, into his target of opportunity. The son of a bitch who'd been out to back-shoot him staggered sideways toward the street and landed facedown in a watering trough with a mighty splash. Longarm leapt lightly through the shot-out door without bothering to open it. The gunplay had cleared the walk in both directions, of course. But as he stood over the gently bobbing rump of the waterlogged back-shooter in the coffin-size trough, reloading his own pistol, police whistles began to chirp all about, like birds in spring.

But Sergeant Nolan of Denver P.D. didn't look much like a robin as he joined Longarm in front of the notions shop and muttered, "I might have known it was you. Where's that ten-gauge I heard first?"

Longarm pointed with his six-gun before he reholstered it, saying, "He tossed it neatly in the gutter. I think he took one six-gun into that trough with him. The other's yonder, behind that open door that lady's screaming at us from."

Sergeant Nolan called out, "Why are you screaming at us, lady? Can't you see we're the law? This bathing beauty in your horse trough is the one who disturbed the peace with yonder shotgun, right?"

The old notions-shop gal came closer, albeit not too close, as she demanded compensation for her shattered glass and nerves. Sergeant Nolan looked innocent and pointed at Longarm, who ticked his hat brim to the old bat and said he'd pay her out of his own pocket if nobody else would. Then he added, "Eating this apple a bite at a time, we'd best find out who this cuss might have been before we decide who's stuck with the tab for all this fun."

He peeled off his coat and got Nolan to hold it for him before he rolled up his shirt sleeves and reached into the now sort of punch-pink water to haul the dead rascal out by the seat of his pants and the black sateen bandanna around his fool neck. By this time the mostly male crowd of curiosity seekers had edged in considerable. As Longarm dropped the soggy cadaver on the walk and rolled it on its back with a boot tip, a familiar figure in a loud checked suit and porkpie hat joined him and Nolan, notebook in hand, to ask just who'd done what to whom and, if possible, why.

Longarm told Crawford of the Denver *Post*, "I cannot tell a lie. I chopped him down with my little .44-40. After that, your guess is good as mine. I never saw the . . . oops, ladies present, until just now."

Crawford turned to the notions-shop lady to ask if she'd seen the shoot-out. She looked accusingly at Longarm and replied, "Lands' sake, the first thing I knew, this big moose in a brown store-bought suit came crashing through my front window, scared me half to death, and two customers clean ran out my back door!"

29

Crawford chuckled at the picture but might not have written anything down if Longarm hadn't suggested, "You'll want to get the name and address of this fine notions shop right, pard. Had I been caught off-guard with, say, a brick wall to one side and nothing but the open roadway to the other . . ."

So Crawford asked the old gal what she called her shop and how she spelled her own name, and as it sank in that she was about to be immortalized on the front page of the *Post*, she began to grow right fond of Longarm for saving her and those other ladies from a fate worse than death.

Then a black porter from a somewhat seedy little hotel even closer to the stockyards volunteered that the dead man had checked in that very morning under the name of Jones, giving his hometown as Steamboat Springs, which inspired Crawford to snap his fingers and say, "Of course! Signing in as a Jones must have strained his brain enough, and he didn't think his hometown was wanted by the law. So it's my educated guess, Longarm, that you just now caught up with the one and original Steamboat Saunders, a lethal lad whose gun hand rents by the hour."

Nolan brightened and said, "Oh, sure, I've heard of Steamboat Saunders in connection with more than one sudden death in this here Centennial State."

Longarm shrugged and said, "I'd say he caught up with me, whoever he might have been. I was up in Steamboat Springs not long ago, and to tell the truth, this is the first I've ever heard of him."

Crawford explained, "His hometown is the last place you'd want to seek such a murderous young cuss, Longarm. He commenced his wild career up there a good three years ago by gunning another old boy in church, from behind. The reason it took me this long to put that pasty face and that black charro outfit together was that he hasn't been too active in Colorado of late, Sergeant Nolan notwithstanding."

30

Nolan waved as he spotted the horse-drawn meat wagon from the city morgue coming around the corner. As he did so, he growled at Crawford, "Where has he been hiding out all this time, then, if you're so smart?"

Crawford answered simply, "Over in the Indian Nation. He hasn't been hiding out. The Indian police have no charges against him. He's always been careful about who he's gone after, until today. They say he put away at least three men for pleasure, and half a dozen for pay. I wonder which he had in mind just now."

Longarm grimaced and said, "We'd never met before, so it couldn't have been personal, as personal as I took the notion. You wouldn't know just where in the Indian Nation old Steamboat squatted betwixt jobs, would you, pard?"

Crawford nodded and said, "Sure I would. They say he was thick with some old Osage squaw in or about Pawhuska, where the tribal council holds its meetings. But what difference does it make now that he's in no shape to pester anyone anymore?"

Longarm answered bleakly, "I haven't killed the cuss who hired him to kill me yet. So I'd best get to work on that."

Chapter 4

The sun was almost down behind the Front Range just to the west of town, but Longarm was still worried that the storefront he was standing in wasn't shaded enough as he watched old Clayburn, the federal prosecutor, coming down the granite steps across the street. But the dapper young cuss never even glanced Longarm's way, and as he rode off in the hansom cab he'd hailed with his fool walking stick, Longarm cut across through the evening rush hour, and to hell with any horse apples he might have otherwise worried about. For he knew he was testing the patience of Clayburn's receptionist indeed. Yet there was no way in hell to get at her without her boss knowing about it, before her damned boss left for the damned day, right?

Once inside he took the marble steps two at a time, sickly certain he'd wind up panting at her office door only to discover she'd locked up and gone home home already. But while the perky brunette looked sort of worried and red eyed she was still there, just, as he popped in on her.

She was standing by her desk, pinning on her summer hat of painted straw and fake fruit as he joined her, and she looked so yummy with both elbows up like that and her summer-weight bodice so tight in that position that it seemed just natural to take her in his arms and kiss her good, so he did.

She kissed him back, with considerable skill as well as enthusiasm. But as they came up for air she gasped, "Why, Custis, what's gotten into you! I'd just about decided you'd forgotten our dinner date and . . . don't you think you'd best let go of me if we're ever going to get out of here this evening?"

He kissed her again but resisted the impulse to explore her further with his hands as he explained. "Change of plans. First let me raise the shade of yonder window so's an Oriental pal of mine can see we're up here, waiting on the pork lo mein and orange gai pan I told 'em we might want if you were still here."

She laughed incredulously and demanded, "Are you suggesting we have dinner, a Chinese dinner, here in this office for heaven's sake?"

He nodded and said, "I ain't suggesting, I'm saying; and it's for your sake, not heaven's, that I dasn't run you home before it's good and dark outside and I know the coast is clear."

"You mean, you think I'm in danger?" she asked him, wide-eyed.

He raised the window shade, spotted young How Chin's friendly wave and speedy footwork across the way, and hauled the shade back down, all the way, saying, "That's better. It's more likely me, not you, they're after. I'm putting all the cards on the table up front so's you can just light out right now, if you'd rather."

As he'd sort of hoped, she wasn't about to do any such thing before he'd satisfied her curiosity and mayhap other appetites. So he told her truthfully about the shoot-out he'd been in earlier. The only thing he fudged on was the way he'd waited across the street until her boss had left. He said, "It's a shame old Clayburn's gone for the day. He no doubt has the only key to your files, right?"

She said she had her own key to the file room, if it was really important. He said, "I'm not sure it is. Let's talk about it after we eat. I wouldn't want to get you in trouble, and it may not be important, anyways."

So naturally he got into the file room and almost got into *her* before How Chin showed up with their dinner pails, and it was just as well; the office was pretty dark by then. For they only noticed after the Oriental delivery boy had spread the swell feed on her desk for them, and left with Longarm's extra tip, that they'd both missed a few buttons covering up for company.

She said she'd never had orange gai pan before and even ate some of it before they somehow wound up back on the leather chesterfield that offered plenty of seating for folk on government business but not much room for passion. She laughed like a mean little kid and said she was sure they'd be caught and fired, if not sent to prison for life, when he spread the leather cushions on the office rug and proceeded to strip her down entire. When she protested that nobody would ever buy the fact that they were working late on legal briefs if they were caught on the floor stark naked, he assured her that no one would ever believe they were doing anything but screwing on the infernal floor to begin with. So she had to agree that that sounded logical, and it sure was fun for Longarm to nibble Chinese food and Maureen, as he'd just learned to call her, at one and the same time. She came up with a way of consuming orange sauce meant for white meat in a manner that belied her first protestations that she'd never in her born days let any man do such wicked things to her.

There was method in Longarm's mad Gypsy lovemaking, aside from how swell it felt to both of them. She was delighted to discover that he was able to bring her to full climax again and again, once he'd gotten his second wind. He was glad he'd asked his Chinese pals to make the tea stronger and blacker than they usually brewed it. For even though he was way bigger and stronger than the passionate receptionist, he'd have wanted to fall asleep with her when

34

at last she rolled onto her bare tummy and began to snore sweetly with him still in her, dog style.

He finished that way, as any healthy man would have, amid such pleasant surroundings, and then he gently withdrew, covered her up with his coat, and smoked a cheroot all the way down to make sure she was out for a spell before he got up, naked as a jay, to pad back into the file room on his bare soles and do things right this time.

Knowing that no matter how fond they might be of each other, and no matter what you got them to promise, the three swiftest means of communication were still telegraph, telephone, and tell-a-woman, Longarm had told her he only wanted to see if they had anything pending on the late Steamboat Saunders. There hadn't been word one on the young hired gun. Clayburn had some of the usual fliers on the James–Younger clan, of course, but nothing on Adeline Dalton née Younger. Longarm wasn't surprised. He found the brief on the pending trial of Wee Willy Wiggins. He ducked into Clayburn's inner office with it and made sure the shades were down before he lit a bitty desk lamp and sat bare-assed in the prosecutor's chair to go over the whole rough draft. He was yawning long before he'd finished. The various depositions by various witnesses neither clashed enough to weaken Clayburn's brief, nor matched so close as to arouse suspicion of a frame-up. There was nothing pointing to anyone but the accused runt and convicted sex offender, save for the simple fact that Longarm couldn't picture one brain being so slick and so stupid at the same time.

The kidnapper had obviously known his victims well, down to how much Hamish Ferguson had had in his bank account and how much he valued his wife. There were even a couple of tintypes on file, showing that the murdered couple had been fairly ordinary-looking folk, the wife mayhap a good deal younger than the Indian agent but hardly a raving beauty. It made Longarm feel even more sorry for the poor cuss. Plain folk who loved each other likely had

35

better reasons than most for their warm feelings.

Knowing to the bottom line how much old Emma would be worth to her Hamish, the kidnapper had abducted her from the Indian agency without being spotted. Clayburn himself had noted that the Shoshone all about would have noticed a total stranger, red or white, while someone who'd been by the trading post a time or two, as Wee Willy had, could likely slip in easily enough. Getting the gal out would have taken more doing. The dead gal's dying words failed to say whether she'd been kidnapped at gunpoint or carried off, say, unconscious and wrapped up in a rug like Cleopatra. Her dying words were paraphrased, of course. The deputy who'd come upon her breathing her last by her dead husband hadn't taken her exact words down in shorthand. But the sheriff up yonder had cross-examined him well enough for anyone reading his account of the conversation to assume he'd gotten it pretty close to what she'd been trying to tell him.

Wee Willy's denials, belied by the simple fact that he'd stopped at the reservation trading post more than once, only served to explain why he'd felt called to gun both the Fergusons once the ransom had been paid. For even if he hadn't ravaged the poor, plain Emma, she and her husband would have both been able to identify him.

So why had such a slick killer, however ruthless, been dumb enough to ride a pony with a mismatched shoe all the way from the scene of his crime to the cathouse he'd been caught in? Hadn't any of the other crooks he'd doubtless met in prison told him a thing about throwing the law off your trail? And assuming the miserable little shit had just been stupid, how did the late Steamboat Saunders fit in?

The door to the inner office opened. Longarm knew better than to cover up as Maureen came over, sleepy-eyed but obviously ready for more. As she moved around to seat her bare behind in his naked lap, she asked him what he was up to back there. He only had to move his bare butt in the swivel chair a mite to assure her he wanted to be up her

36

back there, and so she giggled and leaned forward with her elbows on the desk and her bare feet on the floor, sliding up and down his renewed inspiration in a delightful way, saying, "Oh, I see you got out the Wiggins brief. Are you still working on that case, darling?"

He answered truthfully, since he saw he had to. "Someone connected with that killing up along the Yampa seems to be working on me, honey lamb. Steamboat Saunders hails from Steamboat Springs, Colorado, just a spit and a holler from the scene of the Ferguson kidnapping and killings."

She arched her spine more and murmured, "Faster . . . it feels so fine when you really let go with me! Why would that nasty little Wiggins want you dead, now that he's been caught and charged, dear?"

He braced his elbows on the arms of the chair and began to move in her as he replied in as conversational a tone, "He'd have no sensible reason at this late date. My boss already pointed out that neither I nor any other deputies from around here had any part in the arrest. We only brought him back to stand trial in federal court because Hamish Ferguson was a federal employee. That shoot-out this afternoon works two ways. Could we hold the thought and finish this right? I'm fixing to come in you some more."

She said that made two of them and agreed it felt better, or at least different, to finish face-to-face with her rollicking rump bouncing on her boss man's desk blotter. But once she'd climaxed again, she pleaded, "Take it out before we get horny again, you big goof! Even if the night watchman doesn't catch us in the act, he's sure to wonder if we leave this office much later!"

Longarm started to mention a nearby hotel with a night clerk not half as nosy. But he was no fool, and he had a train to catch well this side of dawn. So he allowed he'd have mercy on her if she'd rustle him up carbon copies from more than one case he hoped they'd have on file.

Later, leafing through the results in an eastbound caboose,

37

he suffered some wistful thoughts about that rinky-dink hotel and all the positions he'd never gotten around to with old Maureen. For although her boss was just as bad as Billy Vail about having everything typed up in triplicate or worse, Maureen hadn't given him anything on the Ferguson case he found surprising, and they hadn't had anything on either Adeline Dalton née Younger of the Osage Strip or the late Steamboat Saunders. So that brush with the hired gun still worked either way, and now there was yet another gal where he worked who'd be able to say wicked things about him, and it hadn't made him feel a lick better about that when Maureen had confessed she'd been dying to find out if it was true he was built tall all over.

Chapter 5

Folk in other parts tended to picture Kansas as flat and covered with sunflowers. A heap of Kansas was, but that wasn't where they'd put Coffeyville. It lay in the Verdigris Valley, between the aptly named Flint Hills to the west and the Ozark foothills to the east, and, being a mite east of longitude 100°, it got enough rain for the natural ground cover to consist of fairly tall timber, now mostly second-growth blackjack oak and cottonwood, where it hadn't been cleared for hardscrabble homesteads.

Before that, it had been cleared of Osage in the interests of neat boundary lines and the Missouri Pacific Railroad. The hitherto free-ranging Osage had been ranging a mite too far from their more numerous Lakota cousins on the northern plains to have a hell of a lot to say about it when the Great White Father lumped them with the other so-called Civilized Tribes of the Indian Nation and moved them south into their own strip.

Thrown open to white settlement as well as railroading, Coffeyville now sported two banks, along with other more reputable businesses, such as cathouses, saloons, and such. Longarm had of course passed through before. So he knew where to order a decent bowl of chili con carne and wash the same down with some strong black coffee before he went to pay the usual courtesy call on the local law.

Being that it wasn't the seat of Montgomery County, Coffeyville rated only an undersheriff to uphold Kansas law and a deputy marshal of Longarm's own rank and seniority to fret about federal statutes that might be threatened by the nearby Indian Nation.

Longarm had neither the time nor the inclination to enter into a popularity contest, so, knowing Kansas was likely less interested in his mission than a possibly proud and proddy gent running a half-assed federal office, Longarm ambled into the one-room lean-to attached to the Coffeyville Post Office to nip any possible misunderstandings in the bud.

He saw right off that there were some to nip. Henry, back in Denver, had wired the U.S. Marshal's Office in Independence, assuming it was was up to them to notify their branch offices.

They hadn't. So the crusty cuss behind the desk in Coffeyville—even older than Billy Vail, albeit not getting paid a lick more than Longarm—was mighty pissed, and said so when Longarm presented his John Doe warrant and other credentials.

But since the old gent, even though pissed, was polite enough to offer a guest a hardwood chair, Longarm felt obliged to smooth things over. "Our clerk is one of them high-school graduates who doubtless sits down to pee, Deputy Slocum. I distinctly recall Marshal Vail instructing him to wire you by name, but you know how hard it is to get good help since the war."

The older lawman growled. "Damned A! These young squirts coming aboard these days don't know what it's like to pull a barbed arrow out of your rump and file a single copy in blood." Then he brightened and added, as it sank in, "You say Marshal Billy Vail hisself knowed it was me in command of this here outpost?"

Longarm didn't like to lie outright when he could avoid it, so he nodded and replied, "I could have told old Billy, had he asked, that they'd never put anyone here in Coffeyville but an old pro with plenty of savvy about the Owlhoot Trail. Being you can't be more'n five miles north of the Osage Strip, you must get all sorts of shady gents of various complexions passing through, right?''

Old Slocum nodded, trying to look modest as he said, ''Damned A! The infernal Indian police run what amounts to a holy sanctuary for white boys wanted in other parts, and as for bad breeds, or white crooks willing to swear to a drop of Injun blood, forget it!''

Apparently having forgotten he was supposed to feel insulted, the older deputy slid a desk drawer open, hauled out a jam jar that wasn't exactly filled with jam, and confided as he poured the white lightning, ''We can't get the warrants outten our federal court that good old Judge Parker issues the deputies working the Cherokee Strip. They say he's riding for a fall with the Eastern do-gooders, who are putting bad things about him in the newspapers.''

Longarm took the hotel tumbler of corn liquor he'd been offered and answered as he raised it to his lips, ''Here's to Isaak Parker, anyway. What's a little thing like due process when those same Eastern assholes set things up to give the outlaws all the advantages?''

Then he held his breath and tried not to cry outright as the Christ-awful moonshine ran down his throat smooth as molten pig iron.

Old Slocum didn't notice. His own eyes were squeezed shut in agony as he swallowed his own liquid fire. Longarm got his breath back and wheezed. ''Smooth stuff. I take it we're drinking the same, lest some poor benighted Indian hurt hisself with it?''

Slocum said, ''You take it right, old son. We confiscated a wagon load of these here jars off an old boy who never saw fit to pay the revenue and still meant to peddle it to the Osage at double the price of properly licensed and bonded bourbon, ain't that a bitch?''

Longarm held his glass up to the light to regard the contents soberly as he replied, "Well, I don't see anything nasty as a wriggle worm or used rubber floating in this murksome stuff. But are you sure it's safe to use as, say, paint remover?"

Slocum chuckled fondly and said, "I never serve stuff I seize unless I knows the bootlegger personal. This shit's only a hundred proof and mostly made from sour mash as wouldn't sicken a hog afore they throwed in the ginger, red pepper, gunpowder, and such. You know they have to flavor trade liquor like that afore the Injuns will accept it as real firewater. I mind a Comanchero whiskey drummer one time as got his balls cut off for serving his customers pure four-star brandy as a special treat."

Longarm had sipped enough of this particular treat to be polite. So he reached for a smoke as he said, "Belle Starr and her clan in the Cherokee Strip are pushing shit that makes this stuff taste at least four-star. But that's up to Isaak Parker to settle betwixt now and the time the limp-wristed reformers drum him out of office. I don't have to tell an old hoss like you why I'm packing some blank warrants to be filled in after I find someone down in the Indian Nation worth hauling out. But this moonshine has put me in mind of at least one in-law of the James and Younger boys that I'm hoping to catch up with, down around Pawhuska. You wouldn't know a dealer in firewater answering to the handle of Lew Dalton, would you?"

Old Slocum laughed and said, "Sure I would. Him and his brood of brats used to live right here in Coffeyville, and it's an insult to most bootleggers to call that white-trash cuss a dealer in firewater. I'm sure he just spikes the contents of his chamber pot with rusty nails, busted glass, and such."

He sipped some of the moonshine he approved of and added, "Didn't know he was kin to Jesse James, though."

Longarm explained, "Dalton's not, directly. His wife, Adeline, is Cole Younger's aunt and, near as I can figure from the notes Billy gave me, a first cousin to Frank and Jesse's mamma, Zerelda Cole, as she was known before she married Lord knows how many men of low repute in a row.''

Deputy Slocum said, "Well, I never. That explains the sticky fingers of the Dalton kiddies, then. Lew and Adeline had fifteen of the little shits by the time they drifted here from Missouri by way of other parts of Kansas.''

"All bad apples, eh?" asked Longarm as he struck a match for his cheroot. But old Slocum shook his head and said, "Fair is fair, and it's too early to say about the gals and younger boys. The reason I finds it surprising that old Adeline is the one with outlaw kin is that she ain't never been accused of anything but having at least a few shitty kids by a total shit. Lew Dalton's a hard-drinking, light-working drifter who's too lazy to make it as a farmer and too stupid to make it as the natural big shot he'd like you to think he is. One of his nine boys, an older one called Frank, seems willing to put in a day's work for an honest dollar. The devil's pick of the litter, young Bob, seems destined to cut someone's throat with a razor before he ever learns to shave with it. The others are sort of in between. They can turn out halfways decent or as bad as their cousin, Cole Younger, depending on whether they listen to Frank or Bob. I sure wish you could take young Bob back to Denver with you. Might save all the other apples in poor old Adeline's barrel.''

Longarm asked just how old this dreadful Dalton was, and when old Slocum guessed at thirteen or fourteen, Longarm was forced to say he doubted the Denver District Court would hang anyone quite that young.

Slocum insisted, "They say Billy the Kid kilt his first man at the age of twelve, don't they?''

Longarm grimaced and said, "I've heard the story. I have my doubts. If the truth be known, I don't even have a proper charge to arrest either parent on, as long as they don't bite me on the leg or bullshit me. I take the tale of knowing where Frank and Jesse are hiding with a grain of salt as well. Would you like to hazard an educated guess as to just

43

who might have tipped my office off to such an unlikely hideout for the Daltons' distant relations?''

Slocum shrugged, said he hadn't even known Longarm was coming, but asked, "How come you finds it so unlikely, Longarm? If Adeline is kin, Frank and Jesse James would trust her afore they'd trust anyone else in these parts, right?''

Longarm shook his head and answered, "These parts are what those Show-Me boys from Missouri would have a tough time swallowing. The Indian Nation was a swell place for a white outlaw to hide out in the days of old U. S. Grant and the notorious Indian ring. Since Hayes has been in office, federal lawmen like Judge Parker have been keeping an eye on both the tribal councils and their guests. Whether or not she ever entertained the James—Younger gang en masse when she was still Belle Shirley, Belle Starr for sure hasn't had any of the gang as houseguests since the North-field raid. Judge Parker's boys dropped by before any of the rascals could have made it down from Northfield.''

He blew a thoughtful smoke ring and added, "I can't see Jesse this far west of his own dear mamma, either. Frank, maybe. But, betwixt raids into other parts, Jesse's always been a sort of home boy, and I've a bet with Billy Vail that when they get him, it won't be all that far from the old homestead outside Liberty, Missouri.''

Slocum drained the last of his heroic drink, still managing to sound sensible as he opined, "You could be right. You could be wrong. They say the Pinkertons report on it ever' time old Zerelda uses her outhouse. 'Course, that ain't saying her baby boy ain't shitting just over the hill or, like your informant wired Billy, anywhere in or about the Osage Strip.''

Longarm asked if they had anything on the late Steamboat Saunders.

Slocum slid open another desk drawer and hauled out a manila folder stuffed with sheets of yellow foolscap. He removed only one sheet and handed it across to Longarm, saying, "That Colorado killer was wise enough to stay out

44

of dutch with us or the Indian police during his stay in the Osage Strip. We naturally kept an eye on him in any case, and seeing we'll never get to arrest him now, you might as well have this otherwise useless list of his knowed associates in these parts."

Longarm took the typed list with a nod of thanks and quickly scanned it before he noted, "Nothing here connecting old Steamboat with anyone named Dalton, let alone James or Younger."

Slocum said, "I'd keep that list and memorize it, anyway, were I in your boots. You're the only lawman within a thousand miles as had a thing to do with the recent death of Steamboat Saunders, and you'll note he had a heap of knowed associates in these parts."

Longarm grimaced and said, "I had to gun the silly son of a bitch. He was out to back-shoot me, for whatever reason."

To which Slocum soberly replied, "That's what I mean. Saunders hung out with a passel of like-minded saddle bums who might think they've plenty of reason to back-shoot *you* now."

Chapter 6

Less than an hour later Longarm had lugged his McClellan and possibles from the railroad baggage shed to the Hehaka Livery & Corral. He draped the saddle over a corral pole and peeled off his tweed coat to hang it on the upthrust butt plate of his Winchester. Then he hauled a cheroot out of his vest pocket and lit it carefully, with both hands cupped around the match head. For though the day was turning to a scorcher, a fairly stiff breeze was blowing up the valley from the south.

The cantankerous old Osage breed who demanded top dollar for the top mounts for sale or hire in Coffeyville let Longarm smoke a spell but broke cover once the tall deputy swung himself up to perch in comfort on that same corral pole. Once he had, old Hank Hehaka grumped over to ask whether Longarm had come in peace or war. Longarm stared off into space a spell, removed the cheroot from betwixt his teeth to study the glowing tip as if he'd never noticed it was on fire before, and replied, "I have to do some riding, down Pawhuska way. They tell me you know how to tell a horse from a hole in the ground, and I got some hills to top and some brush to pop. Might you have a *tasunke* or more that could get me and my gear from hither to yon and back?"

Hehaka came close to smiling as he answered, "One pony, one *good* pony, is best for riding alone among wooded hills where water is no problem. I have a Tennessee Walker we call Sapatonka if you want to talk about money."

Longarm shrugged and said, "I ride for the government as a U.S. Deputy. You likely know Uncle Sam figures two bits a day is enough to hire a Kentucky Derby winner. But I can likely put an extra day or so down on my charge account if you'd like to show me this big blackie of your'n."

This time the old gent let some tooth stumps show as he answered, "*Hoka hey*! Your Osage is terrible, but at least you try, and how do you feel about five dollars a week and a fifty-dollar deposit?"

Longarm chuckled fondly down and answered, "Awful. I learned the little I know of your lingo scouting for the army that time your Lakota cousins went *witco* up in the Pahasupa in the summer of '76. I can see now why the army had to whup *your* red asses earlier."

Hank Hehaka drew in his paunch to stand taller as he rumbled back, "That is a fucking lie! We were never beaten by the yellow legs, never! We never even *fought* them. That is why so many were left when it came time for your Custer to die. We got a better deal than the poor Lakota. You just said, yourself, you were riding into the Osage Strip. Hear me, we got way more land out of Washington than anyone but the eastern pets of the B.I.A. We got more land than the Kansa, Ponca, Oto, Pawnee, Iowa, and Fox put together. Hear me, our strip is bigger than the reserves the Wichita, Shawnee, or Seminole got. The damned old Cherokee, Creek, Choctaw, and Chickasaw got strips a little bigger because they sucked up to you people, see?"

Longarm blew smoke at the old breed and flatly told him he was full of it, adding, "That new Kiowa–Comanche strip south of Fort Reno is bigger'n your'n, and say what you might about them old boys, they've never been famous for friendly. Are you sure you're not out to bullshit me about horseflesh as well? I've yet to see your famous walk-

47

ing horse, and I know you're full of shit about recent history.''

That sent the old cuss over to the stables and back, sort of war-dancing both ways, but the tall black gelding dancing back across the paddock with him made Longarm almost forget his resolve to keep the damned expenses within reason this time. For, sure enough, the ebony-hided saddle bronc had the gait, even dancing, of the famous type from Tennessee.

Longarm had his reservations about the Tennessee Walking Horse being a downright *breed*, albeit most seemed to look as if they'd had at least one thoroughbred grandsire, without looking quite as stupid.

For unlike the high-strung thoroughbred, good for speed on a flat course and not much else, the Tennessee Walker was bred for brains, or at least the ability to learn, and trained, as its name might indicate, to carry its rider far, wide, and fairly fast over most any sort of country at a comfortable clip. One might say the Tennessee Walker was the sprung carriage of saddle broncs. It wasn't worth shit as a cutting horse, and a hunter or racehorse could likely beat it cross-country for the first few hours. But a Tennessee Walker would get you farther in the end and not all that much slower. For it had been developed to begin with as a means of long-distance travel on the none too gentle trails of the rough-and-ready Cumberlands, and Longarm could see this one was made for the not too different Oklahoma Hills. So he took a deliberate drag on his cheroot and said, "Now that's what me and old Tatanka-Yatanka would call a *tasunke,* and we got a deal if you're willing to settle for five bucks a week and no dumb talk about deposits.''

Hehaka grumbled, "Hear me. I hire out horses, good horses. I don't *give* them away. Who told you Tatanka-Yatanka's real name, damn it? You people are supposed to know him only as Sitting Bull.''

Longarm shrugged and said, "He told me one time,

48

personal, that he thinks Sitting Bull's a mighty dumb-sounding name. Can we get back to dickering about business closer to hand? I have to head south and I ain't got all day."

Hehaka replied, "You don't want to ride due south if you are on your way to Pawhuska. Let me have your hand, your left hand, if you want to talk straight, like a man."

Longarm knew the form. The Osage had lived more like Mandan and other settled-down riverside folk than the free-ranging Lakota, even back in what they all called their Shining Times. But folk as talked about the same lingo had about the same religious notions or folklore. Holding another man's wrist so's you could feel his pulse as he promised could qualify as much as common sense as it could folklore, once you stripped away all the bullshit about spirits. Since Longarm never lied when he didn't have to, and had a clear conscience when it came to dealing with other gents of any race, he was able to give his word he'd return Sapatonka within a week or, failing that, pay a fair price for a dead horse. So Hehaka, noting that the tall deputy's heartbeat neither slowed nor speeded up, no matter what he said, decided, "*Hoka hey,* we got a deal if you agree that a real *tasunke* is worth at least two hundred."

Longarm snorted in disgust and said, "I'm only out to hire me a saddle bronc, not your whole remuda. If you paid fifty dollars for that walker, it must have been many a moon ago. For that nag has to be eight or ten years old if I'm any judge."

The old horse dealer grumbled that Sapatonka was little more than a colt who'd worn his teeth down a mite on the notoriously gritty grass in these parts. They dickered back and forth until Longarm said the brute might be worth forty dollars. Then old Hehaka spat on his palm and held it out. So Longarm did the same, and once they'd slapped wet palms and there was no way a gent could back out, the old breed cackled with glee and said, "I slickered you by half. For to tell the truth, I got that walker off another white boy in a hurry for ten dollars and a twelve-year-old paint. He rid poor Sapatonka this far, lathered half to death, like the devil had been chasing both of 'em for many a mile.''

Longarm cocked an eyebrow and observed, ''It could have been a posse just as likely. You naturally asked this mysterious rider for a bill of sale?''

To which the old breed replied, ''I'm a horse trader, not a damned lawyer. What are *you* concerned about, seeing you packs a badge and rides for law and order?''

Longarm answered flatly, ''Law and order. I got enough on my plate right now without riding into the Indian Nation aboard a stolen pony any previous owner should be able to recognize at a quarter of a mile!''

Hank Hehaka said soothingly, ''Hear me, the *tasunke*'s not an Indian pony. The stranger I got it from rode in from the northeast—from Kentucky, he said. He told me he was bound for Pawhuska to visit kin on the Cherokee side of his family.

Longarm frowned thoughtfully and said, ''He must have been a stranger in these parts if he thinks he has Cherokee kin in the Osage town of Pawhuska. What this poor mixed-up youth look like?''

Hehaka shrugged and declared, ''If he had any Indian blood, I'm the queen of England. He had pale blue eyes and hair a lighter shade of brown than your own. He stood six foot tall or a mite less and wore an outfit more town than country. Said he was a horse trader too. But if he was, he wasn't half as good as me at it. I suspected he might have a few sidelines to account for his fancy frock coat and expensive Morgan saddle. Had a habit of darting his eyes all about and wore his gun low in a waxed holster, if you know what I mean.''

Longarm said, ''I know what you mean. Might we by any chance be talking about a Schofield Smith & Wesson as well as blinky eyes?''

When Hehaka said that sounded about right, Longarm got out his wallet suddenly and said, ''That couldn't have been who it sounds like, and even if it was, he's got one hell of a lead on me. But my dear old boss back in Denver will never forgive me if I don't at least *try*. So let's get me settled up, saddled up, and on my infernal way!''

Chapter 7

Longarm rode down along the Verdigris until, a good six miles inside the Cherokee Strip, he spied a pony trail cutting off to the southwest through the stream-side cottonwood and crack willow. At some time in the past someone had nailed a road sign to the trail-side tree. In more recent times some sportive soul had shot the sign to a shapeless mass of kindling. But Longarm had asked directions back in Coffeyville, and it hardly seemed likely anyone would ever have posted a trail that led nowhere at all.

This one led him and old Sapatonka through a bug-infested alder hell and uphill past many a blackjack oak before it even hinted there might be anything more civilized ahead. But Longarm pressed on, secure in the knowledge that he had plenty of canned beans and tomato preserves, as well as smokes and liquid refreshments, if sunset caught him alone in the tanglewood. The odds were just as good that he'd get to spend the night under a roof in the fairly well-settled Indian Nation.

For the experiment in self-government carved out of the eastern half of the Oklahoma Territory had worked better than some old boys such as Dead-Indian Sheridan had expected and, if the truth was to be told, there had always been more wild whites than wild Indians in the Indian Nation.

The notion had been thought up by old Indian-fighting Andrew Jackson, albeit even the more tolerant Tom Jefferson had expressed some doubts about Indians dwelling east of the Big Muddy in such a changing world. What Jackson had called his Indian Relocation Act, while the Indians had called it the Trail of Tears, had taken place before Longarm's nativity in West-By-God-Virginia, but as well as he could put it together, the five fairly assimilated nations of the Old South had met the white folk at least halfway. So even the act evicting them forever from their towns and country had referred to the Cherokee, Choctaw, Chickasaw, Creek, and Seminole as the Five Civilized Nations.

The Cherokee had led the way in adopting such civilized customs as reading, writing, and chattel slavery, with the other nations following their examples, good and bad, at a more experimental pace. At the time Andy Jackson had decided they were just too durned savage to have anywhere near white trash, the Cherokee were living as middle- to upper-class white country folk, some drinking juleps on the front veranda while their colored slaves got to pick the hornworms off all that tobacco. They'd published their own newspapers, kept their money in their own banks, and, in general, carried on like just about everyone else under Chief John Ross, who'd been seven-eighths white and looked sort of like Abe Lincoln in old tintypes.

So naturally, once the Five Civilized Nations had been frog-marched all the way out here to sink or swim their own Indian way, most of them had just gone on living sensibly, keeping Indian habits that worked best for most any country folk and still lighting their cast-iron stoves with store-bought matches, chopping stove wood with a Green River ax instead of a flint tomahawk, wearing washable jeans instead of greasy breechclouts, and so forth. Longarm would have called a white homesteader who painted his fool self blue and ran about bare-assed because his ancestors back around the time of Caesar had done so a total ass as well. So he was neither surprised nor insulted when, along about sundown, someone coughed politely amid the blackjacks off to one side of the trail, and he turned his head to spy a gent sitting his own pony in the shadows with an army rifle resting politely but thoughtfully across the swells of an army saddle. The gent was dressed more army than Indian as well, albeit with a nickel-plated federal badge a heap like Longarm's pinned to the breast of his army-blue cavalry shirt. The Indian's hair hung down in neat but nonregulation braids to frame his diamond-shaped brown face under the squarely worn black Stetson with a quillwork band. So Longarm knew the cuss had to be Osage. The Osage, like other western nations, had been added as an afterthought and still looked it. A Cherokee's hair would have been cut the same as a white lawman's, and while they still wore some tribal trimmings on their personal outfits, they were picky as Texas Rangers about the way they dressed and acted on duty.

The Indian seemed to be waiting to hear what Longarm had to say for himself. So Longarm stated his name, rank, and business. The Indian considered his words a spell before he replied, politely, "I am called Tom Tallchief, *Sergeant* Tom Tallchief, of the Osage Police. Far be it from me to doubt the word of a total stranger, but might you have any means of backing up your story?"

Longarm nodded pleasantly and said, "I'd be proud to show you any badge and ID if you'd be good enough to note I'm not putting either hand on or about my saddle gun or side arm."

Tallchief nodded soberly and said, "Go ahead. Keep away from that derringer in your vest pocket while you're at it, hear?"

Longarm chuckled fondly and said, "You've got good eyes." Then he hauled his billfold from an inside coat pocket and held it up, open, to flash both his badge and personal identification.

That usually did it. This time the other lawman asked to see his Justice Department warrant, which made him a deputy marshal. Longarm tried not to cuss as he patiently replied, "Nobody carries his fool warrant about with him, old son. Those as worry about such matters have 'em framed and hang 'em on the wall, like a wedding certificate or a high-school diploma, see?"

The Osage did. He smiled boyishly and said, "I was being sneaky. It's as easy to forge one thing as another, and have you ever noticed it's only the rascal checking into a hotel with his neighbor's wife who thinks to pack a wedding certificate along?"

Longarm put his billfold away as he answered with a smile, "Few gents I meet spot this derringer I've got clipped to one end of my watch chain, either. I've been hoping to meet up with another lawman smart as you, Tom. As I just now told you, I'm bound for Pawhuska to look up a whiskey drummer named Dalton. I don't suppose you'd know whether he's there or not, eh?"

Tallchief slid his Springfield back in its saddle boot as he answered grimly, "If I knew for a fact that he was drumming whiskey, he wouldn't be in Pawhuska or anywhere else in this strip. He'd be over in Fort Smith, or wherever Judge Parker put him after his trial. *Heya,* Judge Parker doesn't fuck around with whiskey drummers, red or white!"

Longarm edged his mount farther along the trail, and when he saw that the Indian seemed to accept this, he heeled his mount into a walk again as he said, "I've heard Isaak Parker express himself on such scum. But is that the court you Osage Police deal with, Fort Smith being a good three- or four-day ride from here?"

Tallchief fell in on Longarm's left as he replied, "Hear me, I would spend a week—no, *two* weeks—in the saddle before I would turn an outlaw pale as you over to any other

55

federal judge. Our tribal council hasn't been granted the right to punish your kind. Washington must be afraid we'll bruise white asses in our own rough way. So they say we have to turn such pests over to the nearest white court. How are we supposed to know which one may or may not be closer to Pawhuska? All anyone's ever told us benighted savages is that old Judge Parker hangs 'em high and, *wa*, that is where I take 'em!''

Longarm got out two cheroots as they rode on through the blackjacks a spell. He waited until they'd both lit up and Tallchief had pronounced his store-bought tobacco *wa* as well, before he casually asked if it was safe to assume everyone on the Osage force shared Tallchief's enthusiasm for the current federal regulations against peddling strong spirits to Indians, quickly adding, ''There's a few bad apples in every barrel, and I've seen deputies from my own office get falling-down drunk. I hear you can still get a jar of firewater over to Younger's Bend, a heap closer to Judge Parker's court, if you really want it. I hear Sam Starr saves his good stuff for certain members of the tribal council over that way too.''

Tallchief grimaced and growled, ''*Hoka hey*, all Cherokee are born drunks, and the truth is seldom in them when they are sober. We know about Sam Starr and his white-trash-in-laws. You won't find any such brood in *this* strip. Hear me, my people have not settled down as second-class hoe farmers on land never meant for farming. We were here among these wooded hills and grassy bottomlands before the Five Nations tried to scratch a living from the brick-red dirt out here as they had back east. We Osage didn't try to change as much from the way we'd lived in the Shining Times. When the B.I.A. offered us beef cattle to replace our deer and buffalo, we just said '*Wa hoka hey*' and took up the ways of your cowboys. Playing cowboy is not really that much harder than playing Indian, once they fence you in a little, you know.''

They rode on a ways before Longarm said dryly, ''No

offense, but don't that make it easier, if anything, for a saddle bum, 'or even cow thief of my description, to sort of fade into the local populace of Indians playing cowboy.''

The Indian lawman chuckled dryly and answered, ''*Hoka hey!* The Cherokee were half white and the Seminole were half black before they got out here, and since we Osage are the best-looking people in the world, we've intermarried a heap with the better-looking sorts of white folk. So just who might be one race or the other depends on what the tribal council says, or wants to say, about the matter.''

Longarm nodded and said, ''They tell me Belle Starr had her kids declared Cherokee even though she likes to brag on the eldest daughter being sired by Cole Younger. That's so's they can inherit her outlaw way station in the Cherokee Strip, right?''

Tallchief looked disgusted and declared, ''Cherokee would eat shit if you offered to cut them in on it unlawfully, but I have to admit we've a few mighty pale Osage squatting hither and yon in our own strip. It's a matter of having Osage friends and behaving harmless. Our council doesn't worry much about what folk might or might not have done in other parts. We've noticed how your kind makes up mean things about *our* kind. But hear me, anyone who starts any shit here in our jurisdiction is asking for real trouble.''

''In sum, if Lew Dalton and his brood are dwelling in the Osage Strip, it's with the full approval of their more red-faced neighbors, right?'' Longarm said.

The red-faced Tallchief nodded and said, ''*Hoka hey* and damned A. Speaking straight as one lawman to another, I can't say I've heard anything, good or bad, about the man, albeit the name Dalton stirs up a little dust, somewhere back in the corners of my mind. If anyone by that name had ever done anything bad, or even important to my own people, I would remember it. We Osage are smart as well as pretty.''

Longarm chuckled and asked, ''What about Adeline Dalton's maiden name, Younger?''

Tallchief shrugged and said, ''I know who the Youngers

are. I just told you we weren't stupid. We get copies of the same wanted fliers. I think Belle Starr is full of shit about being an old sweetheart of Cole Younger, and I don't know what this Adeline Dalton looks like.''

Longarm said, ''Seeing she'd be Cole Younger's aunt instead of his sweetheart, her looks don't matter. My office heard she's been in recent contact with more distant kin named James. Your office over to Pawhuska would know better whether anyone named James or even Younger has moved in to punch cows, peddle firewater, or whatever, right?''

Tallchief nodded and said, ''Talk to my maternal uncle, Martin Kruger, when you get to our headquarters in Pawhuska. He speaks with a straight tongue, and one of his wives sorts the mail at the post office across the street.''

Longarm said he'd do that and couldn't help asking if Kruger was an Osage name. Tallchief smiled boyishly and replied, ''It is *now*. Forget what I said about one of his wives. I forgot for a moment how picky all you people but the ones who follow the Book of Mormon are about such matters.''

Longarm assured the Indian he never argued about religion. They rode on a short ways, and then Tallchief pointed out a barely visible break in the wall of second-growth greenery to the south, saying, ''I have to make sure some naughty people haven't rebuilt the still we wrecked down that way a few weeks ago. You are on the right trail to Pawhuska, but hear me, are you carrying a bill of sale on that black Tennessee Walker?''

Longarm allowed uneasily that he'd only hired the mount, informally, from the livery in Coffeyville. Tallchief allowed it was probably all right in that case. But when pressed on the matter, he confided, ''A black gelding much like that one was reported stolen, not long ago, off a sort of tough old Indian trader called Gus Woodson.''

''Just how tough do you boys call tough?'' asked Longarm quietly.

He was neither surprised nor relieved to hear the Osage answer, ''Hear me, we do not squat down to piss. I don't think Gus Woodson does, either. They say he has a black temper and the grit to back it. They say he was very cross when somebody stole his favorite mount, and that he means to shoot the liver and lights out of the thief who did it, if ever they should meet.''

Chapter 8

The sun went down as Longarm and his Tennessee Walker were topping a wooded rise. He wasn't all that surprised. Pawhuska was forty-odd miles from Coffeyville as the crow flies, and save for being as black, old Sapatonka didn't look anything like a crow.

The sky was a mite overcast, and the almanac warned there'd be no moonrise for the next couple of hours. So Longarm felt it safe to assume that bitty dot of light off to his right couldn't be the Evening Star and said so to his mount, adding, "It looks like rain, and the bugs in this tanglewood have already proven they like us both. So why don't we see if they have screen doors or at least some good old citronella bug-stink over yonder."

The gelding was in no position to argue. The cabin with the lantern burning in its window was farther off than it had seemed to be at first, and as the evening breeze had shifted to the north, Longarm—and no doubt old Sapatonka—could smell the place long before they were close enough to hail it. Once they were, Longarm had second thoughts about seeking shelter there. When the gelding stopped unbidden, and tried to go most anywhere else despite Longarm's firm hold on the reins he patted the walker's ebony neck with his free hand and said soothingly, "I smell it,

60

too, pard. Old Mr. Death has been camped here quite a spell if both of us can smell his rotten teeth *this* far off.''

He back tracked his edgy mount a few yards away in the tanglewood and dismounted to tether Sapatonka to a nice pungent slash pine. Then he hauled out his Winchester and told the spooked pony soothingly, ''I'll be back directly, Lord willing, if I don't wind up as dead as that cadaver just up wind of here.'' Then he headed into said wind with a thoughtful round levered into the chamber of his Winchester. He was braced for any number of curs to bark at him, or worse, as he came upon a cornfield and, uncertain how far the long way around might be, forged on toward the lantern light on the far side. He'd seldom met Indians, wild or domesticated, who hadn't kept at least a dozen dogs about the camp or premises. As he went on wading through the half-grown cornstalks, nothing barked at him, however. It was true he was approaching upwind, and the rubbery green leaves of elbow-high early growth didn't rustle worth mention as he eased on through, his Winchester barrel clearing the way. But Indian dogs were still supposed to pay more attention than this after sundown, unless they wanted to wind up stew meat. Indians made pets of any children they had in their vicinity but weren't as sentimental about livestock as whites. They tended to eat any critter that didn't want to make its fool self useful some way.

Longarm froze and almost fired his Winchester when he spied another figure in the cornfield, way this side of the cabin, that went with it. Then he realized what had spooked him, chuckled sheepishly, and said, ''Evening, Mr. Scarecrow. You sure are a realistic son of a bitch. Whoever put you together was more artistical, or superstitious, than most sodbusters of my persuasion.''

Closer in, he saw that the scarecrow's ugly but oddly realistic face had been fashioned of yellowish-gray buckskin, dampened and molded over a wad of something that was like modeling clay. An old black wool hat and some corn silk hanging down like hair completed the illusion for anyone easier to fool than a crow. Longarm doubted all that effort had been worth it. The crows still had over a month to figure this cuss out before the corn it was guarding got ripe enough to go for.

Longarm moved on, breaking free of the cornfield to ease across an ominously open dooryard. He knew that with his dark form outlined by the dark cornstalks he'd just left, he was in better shape for a shoot-out than anyone popping out of that cabin at him now. But it puckered his balls just the same, as he eased across the open space in the dark. He knew he was bending country manners all out of shape by sneaking in on strangers like this, when common sense as well as common courtesy called for a visitor to speak out from, say, easy rifle range and wait for an invite to come closer. But the absence of dogs barking, and the odor of death, told him this might not be the time for common country manners. If it hadn't been for that lamp in yonder window, and the fact that this was an Indian reserve, there'd have been all the earmarks of a nester's cabin recently over-run by Indians. The odor of death was thick enough to cut with a knife now, and despite the breeze, the place seemed quiet as a graveyard after midnight.

It wasn't near that late. As he worked his way closer to the cabin, he spied a beam of lamplight spilling out one end, away from the open window overlooking the veranda and door path. So he decided to peek inside the more discreet way.

Once he'd worked his way around to discover little more than a lamplit loophole cut through the otherwise solid end of the dinky cabin, he automatically took off his hat and shoved an eyeball up to the logs for a look-see.

He saw a nice-looking gal in her mid-twenties seated in a Brumby brand rocking chair with a buffalo robe over her lap and lower limbs. She wasn't rocking. He had to look close to see she was breathing, as well as upright in the stiff-backed chair. Above the buffalo robe she was dressed in a blue-print calico few white farm gals would have sneezed at, but her features and complexion looked full-blood. Tallchief's bragging about his Osage people being pretty had been well taken, albeit the gal inside looked one hell of a lot more kissable than any infernal lawman. By scrootching his head one way and then the other, Longarm was able to see that she seemed to be alone in there as she stared at the inside of her front door, as if expecting visitors.

Longarm eased around to see if there might be a back door. There was, near a woodpile and a wood-ash pile leading to a dinky outhouse by a chicken coop. Longarm knew better than to prowl anywhere near a chicken coop after dark, watchdogs or no watchdogs on the premises. There was a modest barn and some other buildings farther over that way. They were tough to make out in detail in the darkness. Longarm tried easing open the back door. It didn't want to ease. He figured he could kick it in if he had to, but there had to be a better way.

He crawfished back the way he'd come, all the way back to that cornfield, and pulled the scarecrow's single stake out of the moist earth, muttering, "I got somebody else for you to help me scare, Mr. Scarecrow."

The human-size figure made a load more clumsy than heavy, thanks to being mostly bib overalls and an old wool greatcoat stuffed with straw. But the alderwood sapling it had been built around was stout, whittled to a sharp point at the bottom. So when they got to the veranda, in front of the closed cabin door, Longarm was able to spear the whole shebang down hard, between two planks, and step to one side, his Winchester ready as he and the scarecrow waited to see what happened next.

What happened next was that the door flew open and a white-man-dressed cow popped out like a cuckoo-clock bird to blaze away at the scarecrow standing there until Longarm blazed away in turn and blew him sideways off his feet just as yet a second cuss leaned out that lit-up window with his own revolver blazing sort of careless. Longarm put a Winchester round in his head before he could figure out who or what he wanted to shoot at. The gun slick wound up slung head-down across the windowsill above a spreading puddle of blood and brain froth. The first one down lay on his side in a fetal position, so, seeing that the son of a bitch might still be alive, Longarm called out, "Are you still alive, you son of a bitch?"

When that didn't work, he tried calling out to the lady inside the house. When he told her to get her sweet self out here with both hands in the air, she called back, "I can't. They tied me down in this damned chair with rawhide, the mean things!"

Longarm had long since learned to take the word of a strange woman, or even a strange man, with a grain of salt. But without exposing himself to fire from inside, he called back, "I was wondering why a full dressed woman might want such a heavy lap robe, even after dark, in high summer, ma'am. Might I have the honor of addressing the lady of the house, and is it safe to say that these two white boys bleeding on your front veranda don't live here regular?"

She called back, "I never saw them before sunset this very evening. I'm the Widow Tipisota—or Whitehouse, to my English-speaking neighbors. I'd just finished supper here, alone, when the two of them rode in. They called each other Larch and Babe. They said someone was hot on their trail. I can see they were right, if you're the law!"

Longarm didn't answer. He figured it might be just as well to let her, and anyone else in there, assume he was still on the veranda, pondering her words, while he strode quickly around to the loophole again for a second peek at her pretty profile.

She still looked as pretty. But now she'd kicked the buffalo robe off her lap and he could see how they'd lashed her wrists together in her lap and wrapped more thongs across her thighs to keep her down in the heavy rocker. He strode back to the open window, it being closer, and grabbed the dead man's belt, hauling him all the way over the sill and out of the way as he faced the young widow for the first time by the light of her oil lamp on the packing case between them. As their eyes met, hers looked mighty scared, as they no doubt had every right to look, within reason. Longarm smiled reassuringly at her and forked a long leg over the sill to join her inside. He'd naturally allowed the muzzle of his Winchester to proceed him, so when the door of an upright wardrobe popped open, Longarm naturally fired a couple more rounds of .44-40 that way, and a third white man spilled out across the dirt floor. The tied-down Osage gal wailed, "I didn't want to lie like that! He had a gun on me all the time!"

Longarm stepped around her to kick the Navy Colt conversion well away from the third man's still twitching corpse as he muttered, "I noticed. I hope you're not still holding out on me, Mrs. Tipisota."

As he cut her loose with the pocketknife in his free hand, she assured him she wasn't, and that he could call her Martha. She rose, rubbing at her own chaffed wrists, and added, "The one holding out in yonder wardrobe was the leader, I suspicion. They called him Jay Hawk. Funny handle for one of *your* boys, ain't it?"

Longarm cocked an eyebrow at her to demand, "Haven't you ever noticed such a common Kansas term before, being you speak plain American, and Kansas can't be forty miles north of your back door?"

She replied, "Oh, that kind of Jayhawker. My people didn't take sides in the War between the States."

He knew that was a lie for certain. But one could hardly blame most of the Indian Nation for siding with the Confederacy against the very government they owed so much to; and, what the hell, the war had been over for years, and the Indians had paid for picking the wrong side with the loss of more land and even fewer powers of self-government. So he contented himself with saying, "I had the notion long before I got here that someone might not want me to get here. I can't recall seeing any of these young jaspers before, and none of those nicknames rustle any

65

wanted poster in my brain. Your own Osage Police may be able to ID 'em for us if they've been in the Nation for any length of time.''

Again he thought he caught a hint of unreasonable fear in her big sloe eyes before she looked away and said something about putting the coffee on if he'd be good enough to haul all three bodies clear of her cabin. He said, "I can line them up out front, downwind, easy enough. But would you like to tell me first who *else* seems to be dead around here?''

She didn't, or couldn't, meet his eyes as she answered in as innocent a voice as he'd ever heard. "My old yard dog, Wahaha, hasn't been acting right the last few days. Do you reckon he might have died out in the woodlot or amongst the tall corn? Those three saddle bums you just saved me from are the only human beings I can remember dying on this property since my man come down with an ague the winter afore last.''

Longarm sniffed experimentally and told her, "It gets harder to tell for sure, the longer you smell it. When me and my pony picked up the first whiffs, close to an hour ago, we could have sworn we were downwind of the mortal remains of someone dead a lot longer than these three jaspers.''

Then he added, "We live and learn, though. I'll tidy up the remains we can account for the easy way, and then, with your permission, I'll fetch my mount in from the tanglewood. Where might these old boys have left their own riding stock, your barn out back?''

She said she wasn't sure, explaining, "They just came bursting in on me only about an hour before you arrived to turn the tables on them. You go ahead, and meanwhile I'll reheat the Arbuckle. If you're hungry, I can manage some sowbelly and collard greens to go with your coffee and cake.''

He assured her coffee and cake would do him just fine and got to work at his own chores, trying to convince himself that he smelled a dead dog some damned where around here.

He couldn't. As he led his walking horse around the cornfield, almost wide of the sickly sweet smell, he confided, "That's humankind rotting, sure as hell, Sapatonka. It wasn't dogs they detailed us to bury our first summer of the war. You get to where you can tell enlisted men from officers, once their last meal's had some time to ferment in their dead guts. I have yet to smell a dead dog full of grits, greens, and corn liquor, have you?"

The black walker didn't answer. He led it to the barn, where it whinnied into the darkness and got nickered at in return. Longarm struck a match to find that sure enough, there were four other ponies, two mules, and a buckboard in the barn, along with the plow, hay rake, and such the mules hauled across those cultivated forty acres when and as required. He lit a stub candle he found handy and unsaddled the walker to rub it down and put it in a stall beside the other stock before he scouted up some fodder and water. Once he'd found the hand pump out back, and the cracked corn and silage in the tack shed, he watered and then fed the ponies of the three saddle bums as well, having noticed that the three troughs were bone dry as well as empty. The mules had been watered and given plenty of silage earlier. So Martha had likely been telling the truth about them riding in out of nowheres to catch her by surprise around sundown. He wondered if they'd asked her about that funny smell, and what she might have told them. He went back to the cabin to find out.

As he leaned his Winchester just inside the door he called out, cheerfully, "Well, come moonrise I'll hitch up your buckboard and we can run those three fresh cadavers into the nearest settlement before they get to really stinking. That'd be the town of Okesa, ten or twelve miles this side of Pawhuska, right?"

She was standing by her kitchen range on the far side of the cabin as she answered softly, "There's no town law in

Okesa. Just one store that serves as the post office as well. I thought you'd want to spend the night here, at least.''

He hauled the rocker she'd been bound to closer to the packing case the lamp still burned on and sat down, replying truthfully enough as he regarded how nicely her trim figure filled that print calico. ''Under ordinary traveling conditions I'd be more than glad to bed down here even longer. But as a pale-faced lawman I'd look sort of rude if I sat on even one killing any longer than it took to report it to the proper authorities here where we're within Osage jurisdiction, and I haven't even paid a courtesy call on your Indian police.''

She brought him a slab of chocolate cake and a mug of steaming coffee on a bitty tray. As she sat it down she told him softly, ''We both know no Indian police would want to mess with a white marshal, don't we?''

He shrugged and replied, ''I'm only a deputy marshal, and whether they messed with me or not, it's safe to say they'd *want* to, ma'am. Since there's nothing honest lawmen ought to fuss at one another about, as far as I can tell, so far I feel no call to get myself in bad with your Osage law. I got enough on my plate, besides this swell-looking cake, I mean. Ain't you fixing to have any, Miss Martha?''

She replied what she'd said before about those rascals intruding on her just as she'd finished her own supper. She added, ''They made me reheat the last of my leftovers and insisted I eat some more afore one of 'em busted in to say you was coming and they tied me up to use as bait. So forgive me when I say I'm still too filled with butterflies to swallow another bite.''

Longarm followed her drift and reached for the coffee mug. Then she suddenly slapped it out of his hand, and as he watched it bound wetly across the dirt floor, he heard her sobbing, ''Oh, I can't! I just can't! Not after you saved me from Lord knows what wicked fate!''

Then she ran across the cabin and threw herself facedown on the one narrow cot, sobbing fit to bust. Longarm stayed where he was by the packing crate. It wasn't all that large a cabin. He let her sob herself down a mite before he assured her, "Heck, I wasn't about to swallow that much arsenic at a gulp, ma'am. No offense, but you made it so strong, it smelled more like onion soup than coffee. How did you manage that, out here in the tanglewoods. Did you boil down a mess of that Borgia brand flypaper?"

She suddenly raised her head from the bed and asked with a sheepish little smile how he'd guessed. He shrugged and told her, "I'm a lawman. I'm paid to know about such improvisations, ma'am. Seeing you don't want to kill me, after all, don't you reckon it's time you told me about the gent you *did* kill, oh, three or four days ago?"

She swung her bare feet to the floor and sat up, saying bleakly, "I'd better show you why first." Then she simply shucked her print calico over her head, as if they were old pals indeed.

Longarm caught his breath for more than one reason as the lamplight gleamed on her tawny, nude body. She was built even better than he'd imagined, and he'd imagined she'd look swell in the buff. But her beauty was marred by blotches of black and blue, and when she stood up and turned her back to him, he saw that her shapely bare buttocks were crisscrossed with barely healed welts cut into her by a hickory switch, if not a riding quirt. He whistled softly and said, "Forget what I said about you serving arsenic to a *gent*. Then kindly put your duds back on so's I can pay attention when you tell me the whole sad story, from the beginning."

She slipped her print calico back on as she began. "I told you true about my lawsome husband dying natural, a couple of winters back."

As she sat back down on the one bed Longarm rose, stepped over to the stove, and asked, "Whose husband did you serve that arsenic to, in that case?"

She answered simply, "A woman has needs, even if she has the strength and skills it takes to drill in forty acres of cash crop."

Longarm began to put together a pot of coffee from scratch as he observed, "I noticed someone had been keeping your corn tidy with a busy hoe indeed. Was he another Osage, or someone with less right to be here? I've good reasons for asking."

She said, "He was neither your kind nor my kind. He was a good-looking and slick-talking drifter who dropped in on foot this spring with a tale of having just been fired up Kansas way by a mean boss who hated Indians."

Longarm cocked an eyebrow and said, "Hold on. You just said he was neither." Then he went on refilling the pot he'd rinsed out a couple of times already when she explained, "He said he was a breed, even though he was as gray-eyed as you. He might have been. If he was, he had no Osage blood. The few words he knew in what he said was the tongue of his own nation made no sense to me and—"

"Get to where you murdered him," Longarm cut in as he opened a cupboard near her stove to add, "Is this mason jar as looks like it's half filled with honey your store of boiled-down flypaper, ma'am?"

She said it was and continued. "He said he needed a job and I was in the market for a hired hand. So I hired him and, well, I reckon you know how things get once a man and woman spend some time together all alone on an out-of-the-way spread."

Longarm nodded and asked, "How come he took to beating on you if you was, ah, already agreeable?"

She blushed beet red and looked away, half sobbing. "That wasn't what we fussed about. You say you noticed how neatly that corn got hoed this very week. It was me, not him, as hoed it. You see, he did have notions from the Shining Times when it came to what was warrior's work and what was women's work. I told him even Osage men worked hard these days, to make something of themselves in a changing world. He hit me and told me to shut up."

Longarm sniffed some store-ground coffee suspiciously,

failed to detect even chicory in it, and scooped some into the pot as he asked her, quietly, why she hadn't shut up, at least until she could get some help with her new hired hand.

She said, "I tried to get along with him. It didn't work. Once he'd laid hands on me and seen there was nothing much I could do about it, he seemed to find it a grand notion. He found some jars of corn my late husband had stored out back to mellow some. He really roughed me up when he was drunk, too drunk to . . . You know."

Longarm hunkered down to shove some stove wood in under the fresh pot as he mildly objected, "You could have run away, while he was drunk."

But she half sobbed. "Oh, sure, and wouldn't that Maria Pukwanna have a grand bit of gossip to spread about me all the way from here to the Cimarron! Aside from that, he threatened to really hurt me if I told anyone he was here in the Osage Strip. Once he'd been here a spell, he confided he hadn't been fired from any Kansas spread. He never said what he was wanted for in other parts. But he did tell me one night when we were, well, more friendly, that he'd just hate to leave me when the time came, but that leave me he meant to, as soon as some pals he'd written showed up."

Longarm nodded and said, "That accounts for that extra pony in your barn. How did you account for their pal not being here when they showed up this evening?"

She repressed a shudder and said, "I told them he'd gone into town for more liquor and that I was expecting him back any minute. I don't think they believed me. You saw the way they tied me up when they noticed you moving in on 'em."

Longarm sniffed, grimaced, and said, "I see they found your tale of a dead dog about as convincing as I did. Where did you plant their pal, by the way?"

She confided, "Under the compost pile out back. I reckon I should have buried him deeper, eh?"

Longarm smiled thinly and said, "That's for sure. Leftover human don't compost at all like leftover tater peels, coffee grounds, and such. We might be able to save your Osage Police a mighty messy chore if we can ID him for certain as neither Osage nor Wasichu.''

Describing his own race in her lingo set her off in a burst of the same. He laughed sheepishly and said, ''Hold on there, Minnihaha! I know Wasichu means my kind and that nobody who talks your lingo likes to be called a Sioux. But after that I do way better in English. What I meant about this old boy you had to get shed of before his pals showed up described himself as an Indian, but not of the nation this land he's buried in right now might have been allotted to.''

She asked what difference that made. He explained, ''If I take your word you killed a Wasichu for mistreating you, you still have to stand trial in federal court, before a judge and jury of my persuasion.''

She nodded knowingly and replied, ''In that case I feel sure and certain he must have been some breed of trash Indian. Maybe a Cherokee. I sure don't want that Maria bruting it about I got familiar with a damned old Seminole or even a Creek!''

He left the cold pot to perk in its own good time as he moved over to sit beside her on the cot, reaching for a smoke as he told her, ''Creek prefer to be called Muskeegee, and we don't want you answering to the death of anyone who belongs in the Nation at all if it can be avoided. Let's start with the dead rascal's given name.''

She said, ''He told me to call him Ben. His pals asked for him by that handle when they called for him this evening.''

She had no last name to add to a simple handle like Ben. When he pressed her on Ben's claim to Indian blood, she said she'd never heard of his mother's nation, the one time he'd mentioned it. She said it had sounded something like Sissy and agreed that could hardly be it.

He lit the cheroot, handed it to her, and asked how she felt about Tsistsitsah.

72

She brightened, puffed, and answered, "*Hokay hey! That's it!*"

He told her, "Cheyenne. He was likely telling the truth. We call 'em Cheyenne the same as you because it means folk who talk funny in your lingo. Tsitskitsah is what they call their fool selves. Nobody else would bother. If your Ben was part Cheyenne, he had no call to be here in the Osage Strip."

She asked where Cheyenne was supposed to hang out these days, and he told her, "They ranged from Colorado on up to Montana in their Shining Times. The South Cheyenne are supposed to be behaving themselves around Fort Reno, if they're in these parts at all. Since your Ben had gray eyes, it's more likely he was a Colorado rider with a Cheyenne or part Cheyenne mamma. But let's recall him as an Indian and recall what Phil Sheridan always said about good Indians when we report all these dead houseguests to your own law. I can't see 'em making a fuss about the three I just had to gun, them looking like plain old Wasichu to me."

He took his cheroot back and rose to see how the coffee was coming along. As he strode across the dirt floor it sounded as if a big wet frog was keeping step with him on the shingled roof above. From her bed the Osage beauty said, "Oh, it's starting to rain. You'll not want to haul them into town tonight, after all, right?"

He poured them both some strong but safer coffee as he told her, "When you're right, you're right. I'd be a fool to drive a buckboard blind in strange country, even if I was in a hurry. I ain't, seeing those old boys ought to stay fairly fresh overnight in a cool rainstorm."

She took her mug from him with a knowing smile, saying, "Goody. Why don't you trim that lamp and see how well this bitty bed can hold the two of us, then."

He sighed, sat down beside her again, and said, "You'll never know how tempting that sounds, Miss Martha. But I'd be an even bigger fool if I compromised myself with

73

such a lethal lady. So I reckon I will trim that lamp and try for some shut-eye, but, no malice intended, I'm fixing to fasten either your ankle or your wrist to this here cot with my handy-dandy handcuffs first. You being the hostess, I'm letting you decide which way you'd sleep more comfortable, alone.''

Chapter 9

It seemed Osage gals were good at sulking whether a man ravaged and beat 'em or tried to treat 'em downright decent. He didn't even keep her handcuffed as they drove on the next morning with the three bodies riding in the back wrapped in tarps, and old Sapatonka trailing along behind, tethered to the tailgate. He'd told Martha Whitehouse it was up to her own law whether she got to keep the dead men's ponies or not. Meanwhile they were comfortable enough in the barn back yonder. So she was the one doing all the bitching. She was likely riding beside him in considerable discomfort as the day wore on. Every time he offered to cuff her to a tree off the trail so's she could heed any call of nature she might want to, she hissed at him that she didn't want to. They said Queen Victoria hated to admit she ever go pissed, either.

They got into the crossroads settlement of Okesa well before noon. Martha had been right about there being little more than a general store cum post office there. But they had a stout log cabin they used for nasty drunks on allotment days, and the storekeeper doubled as the local justice of the peace as well as postmaster. So when Longarm led Martha inside, ordered some soda pop for the both of them, and explained the canvas-wrapped cadavers out front to the old

Indian, the latter made change, warned one and all he was putting on his JP feathers, and sent his kid clerk to fetch an Osage Police trooper who just might be in town as he took oral depositions from both Longarm and Martha. The hatchet-faced old cuss was as smart as most rural JPs when it came to rough-and-ready law, but Longarm had to explain it twice before the Osage understood that his little sister, as he called her, wasn't under arrest. Once he did, he demanded, ''Why in thunder did you bring my little sister in to me if she's not charged with killing any infernal Wasichu? I mean white boy.''

Longarm said, ''I know what Wasichu means, but I still won't call you a Sioux. Miss Martha witnessed my shootout with the three saddle bums who couldn't have been up to any good.''

The Indian JP grumped, ''I just said I have no jurisdiction over Wasichu on Osage land, cuss their big blue eyes. What do you expect me to do about a Wasichu lawman enforcing the laws against the bastards bothering us?''

Longarm replied, ''I'm glad to agree they're all mine, to keep and cherish. They didn't have a lick of ID between the three of 'em. All I can do is wire an all-points once I get in to Pawhuska, in hopes someone else knows who they might have been and how come they seemed out to get me. They do have a telegraph office in Pawhuska, don't they?''

The JP nodded and growled, ''Of course they have a telegraph office. How do you think we contact Washington when our allotment's overdue, with smoke signals? Hear me, I find those dead boys out front died fair and square in a good fight. I have spoken.''

Martha shot Longarm an uneasy look. He didn't say anything. They'd already told the old JP about the breed, or self-styled breed, she'd murdered for mistreating her. The canny old cuss had caught the look that passed between them. He asked, ''Deputy Long, did you have a proper warrant for that cuss buried under my little sister's compost pile?''

76

When Longarm confessed he didn't and added that the John Doe warrants he had on him only provided for the arrest of white outlaws, the old Osage cackled, "There you go, then. Even you Wasichu recognize the rights of self-defense, as long as it's not one of us defending ourself from one of you, so why don't you let *us* worry about whether my little sister had the right to feed flypaper to an unwelcome pest?"

Longarm chuckled and said, "Come to study on it, they do put that handy mixture of sugar, glue, and arsenic on waxed paper to get rid of unwelcome pests, and far be it from me to argue religion with my elders."

So the old JP nodded soberly at Martha and muttered something in their own soft singsong, and that seemed to be that. The young clerk came back to say something in Osage that sounded dirty, or maybe that was just because of the way he was grinning. The JP nodded, turned to Longarm, and said, "You're in luck. The only Osage peace officer within miles just left for Pawhuska. His girlfriend doesn't expect him back for days, if then. Why don't you just run those dead boys on into town and let me get back to running this infernal store?"

Longarm looked down at Martha, murmuring, "I might have me a tricky transportation problem, now that I see Miss Martha's free to head the opposite way with her buckboard and mule team."

She hesitated, then purred, "I haven't been into Pawhuska to shop in a coon's age, and I reckon I'd feel safer on the road with an escort. So why don't we just combine business with pleasure?"

He said that was jake with him, and they were soon on their way again. But they hadn't gone far when she looked back, saw they had the trail through the tanglewood all to themselves, and pleaded, "Can't we take us a little trail break now, Custis? Now that you've been so sweet about Ben, I'm not mad at you anymore and, well, to tell the

77

truth, I'm just dying to run off in the woods a ways and . . . you know.''

He nodded understandingly and reined the mules off the wagon trace into a grove of blackjack and slash pine, assuring her he felt no call to handcuff her in such an undignified position. She blinked at him in confusion, caught on, and laughed like hell.

When he asked how come, she leaned in closer to confide in him, or warn him, ''I don't have to take a leak, you fool. It's been almost two full years since any man I really liked got into my poor, lonely ring-dang-do, and I've been dying to screw you silly since first you shot your way into my life, you handsome brute!''

Chapter 10

The slash pines offered a pleasant smell, and the blackjack oaks provided deep shade a hundred yards off the wagon trace. But it was close to high noon, and not a leaf was stirring in the sticky summer air amid the second-growth weed trees. It only felt a mite cooler at first, when Martha helped him shuck his duds after beating him to bare-assed easy. Once she had him naked, too, his suggestion that they take it easy and make it last in this infernal heat fell on deaf ears, and he soon felt hot and sweaty, even with her on top doing most of the work. The rain the night before had kept the bugs at bay as he'd dozed in Martha's cabin with his duds on, plenty of tobacco smoke in the air. But as if to pay him back for it now, something creepy-crawly sank its pincers into his bare rump, and as he thrust it skyward from the moist forest duff, Martha took it as a compliment and moaned, "*Hoka hey!* Faster! Faster!" So he tried to kill that son of a bitching ass-biter with his ass by pounding the earth under them with it, and she got too excited to talk English as she moaned and groaned atop him. But he followed her drift as she climaxed, more than once. For a lady and a tiger sounded much the same when it was coming, no matter what its mother tongue.

After they'd climaxed together the third time, with him

on top to finish right, Martha stared dreamily up at him
from her halo of unbound raven hair to marvel, "That was
even better than I expected, as soon as I noticed how tall
you were down yonder. Do you like the way it feels in my
ring-dang-do, darling?"

He said he sure did, and when another bug bit him in a
manner designed to make him thrust unexpectedly, she
gasped and pleaded, "Have a little mercy, will you?"

He laughed, explained it had been as much a piss-ant as
passion, and groped in his nearby duds for a cheroot and
matches, adding, "We have to get some smoke going here,
if only in self-defense. Do you reckon your folk invented
smoking because they noticed it kept bugs at bay?"

She said she didn't know her own kind had invented
smoking and insisted, "I was taught we got all our bad
habits from you Wasichu. Nobody drank firewater or kissed
a girl's ring-dang-do afore you fresh boys moved into our
neighborhood, you know."

He lit the cheroot and rolled off to blow smoke down
between them before he confided, "We taught you to drink,
you taught us to smoke, and I doubt even Professor Darwin
will ever figure out who invented eating pussy, bless his or
her hide."

She murmured, "Pussy? I thought you Wasichu called it
a ring-dang-do, darling."

He laughed and said, "I doubt we have time to repeat
every name such delights have ever been called, seeing as
we want to get to Pawhuska sometime this afternoon."

She snuggled closer and asked him to try. He lay on his
back in the forest duff, blowing smoke up through the oak
leaves above them, and after he'd repeated no more than,
say, fifty terms for her sweet little ring-dang-do, he sang
that old song about the same in a low and not at all lewd
tone.

"When I was young, and in my teens,
  I met this gal in New Orleans,

> For she was young, and pretty, too,
> > And let me play with her ring-dang-do!''

Martha thought it was a swell song. So he went on singing and blowing tobacco smoke as she began to blow on something else in a manner suggesting she really didn't want to hear the end of the dumb song. So he'd have stopped in any case if, just as they were getting to the part about going down to her daddy's cellar and her telling him he was a nice young feller, that Tennessee walker, tethered just out of sight, hadn't nickered, as if happy to see some old pal.

Longarm went on singing, albeit softer, as he gently lifted the Indian gal's pretty face from his lap and signaled her with his eyes. She'd heard Sapatonka's gentle warning, of course. But at first she stared at him as if he was a real Wasichu Witco, or Crazy White Man. For he went right on singing as he eased away from her to get at the gun rig he'd placed atop his balled-up duds just in case something like this ever happened.

Martha caught on as he rose, stark naked save for the six-gun in one big fist and softly crooning.

> ''You naughty girl, her mother said,
> > You've gone and lost your maidenhead,
> > > There's only one thing left to do,
> > > > Go advertise your ring-dang-do!''

He sang even softer as he signaled the naked gal to stay put on her pretty bare butt, and commenced to ease away from her on his bare feet. The forest duff was damp and mostly noiseless, thanks to that rain the night before. When he did put the ball of a foot down on anything brittle enough to crunch, he was able to avoid doing so, thanks to his bare soles. Walking pussycat-style wasn't all that tough when one wore the same sort of footware.

The man or beast that had inspired Sapatonka to nicker was trying to move as quietly, without much luck, as Longarm cocked an ear to judge the direction of a snapping twig and, having done so, eased himself around the far side of an oak, softly crooning.

"So she went to the city to become a whore,
 She hung a sign above her door,
  One dollar now, and the rest when through,
   That's how she sold her—

"Freeze, you son of a bitch!"

But the ragged-ass white man he'd spotted bulling through the tanglewood his way didn't freeze. He raised the six-gun in his left hand, searching wildly for the source of Longarm's command with his hat-brim-shaded eyes. So Longarm fired low, folding the rascal at the belt line like a jackknife before he moved in, muttering, "It's about time I took one of the bastards alive!"

But despite being gut-shot the gun slick he'd dropped amid the second growth still seemed to have some fight left in him, or perhaps the sight of anything the size of Longarm bearing down on him in broad-assed daylight buff naked convinced him he was only enjoying a nightmare. At any rate, he raised his Remington .44 again to fire, and naturally Longarm fired first.

Longarm aimed for the wounded gun slick's left shoulder, not wanting to damage the goods any further, but Ned Buntline's penny dreadful magazines to the contrary notwithstanding, it's not really that easy to hit a writhing human target *anywhere*, and so Longarm's second round hit just to the left of the rascal's heart and inspired him to wail, "Now you've done it! I'm kilt for certain, and they told me you were all wind, damn their eyes!"

Longarm moved closer, kicked the fallen man's six-gun out of sight among the undergrowth, and hunkered down beside him to reply, "You may be right, old son. I'd be proud to fix 'em for getting you in this dumb fix, if only I knew who they might be."

The gut-shot man with the hulled lung stared glassy-eyed and replied, "A lot you know about this child's brains, Longarm. I'd have to be dumb as hell to peach on my own pals to a lawman as just now kilt me, bare-assed. How come you snuck up on me bare-assed, Longarm?"

The naked deputy chuckled down at his victim and murmured, "The better to sneak up on you, my dear. You're right about my killing you. So if you'd like us to ship your remains anywheres in particular, you'd best speak up."

The dying man grunted and replied, "Ain't been nobody gave a hang about me since my dear old momma died, save for a nice young thing I met in Dodge when everyone was younger and prettier. She used to let me have it free when I was short of money. So she must have liked me at least a little, don't you reckon?"

Longarm nodded soberly and said, "They say even old Jesse has a pretty little wife who's true to him, and anyone can see you were a much nicer cuss. Where is old Jesse, these days, by the way?"

The glassy-eyed owl-hoot rider muttered, "Up near K.C. or maybe St. Joe, so they say." Then his glassy eyes got wider as Martha joined them, naked as Longarm, to ask, "Who is he, or was he, dear?"

Longarm said, "I'm working on that. Old son, this naked lady would be Martha Whitehouse of the Osage Nation. I disremember what you said your name was."

The dying man blew bloody bubbles, coughed, and softly managed, "Howdy, Miss Martha. You can call me Green River Roy. I wasn't sent to gun *you*. They offered me five hundred to gun this bare-assed boyfriend you've took up with. As you can see, we all makes mistakes."

Then he laughed, blew some more bubbles, and went lifeless as a wet dishrag. Longarm felt for a pulse, anyway, before he sighed and told her, "I wish you'd come sooner. At least we got a name and you heard him admit he'd been hired to gun me, personal. The only way it works is that he found out in Coffeyville I'd left there to head down here, and naturally they'd have told him back in Okesa that he'd just missed us.''

He closed the dead man's eyes and rose, gun in hand, to add, ''Had not it been for your ring-dang-do and that dumb old song, he'd likely have gone on all the way to Pawhuska, where he'd have been waiting on me with a much better edge, bless you and your ring-dang-do!''

She dimpled prettily and replied, ''I told you it was good for something, didn't I? What position would you like to try next?''

He laughed despite himself and said, ''For openers I'd best put my pants and boots back on, at least, before I scout up this dead rascal's pony and load his dead ass aboard your buckboard with those others.''

She pleaded, ''Can't it wait just a few more cotton-picking minutes, sweetheart? *My* ass ain't feeling dead at all. I suspicion all this excitement's got my passions gushing again!''

He started to tell her not to be silly. Then he wondered why he'd want to say a silly thing like that. For there they were, still stark naked, and damned if he didn't feel up to a little more gushing his own fool self. So in the end it was after sundown when they finally rolled into Pawhuska in hopes of getting back to serious business.

Chapter 11

The Osage capital, Pawhuska, had been built along the southwest bank of the Bird River, a heap wider than deep this time of the year, with the approval of the Great White Father to function as something between an Indian agency and a county seat, the Osage being encouraged to run their strip along the lines of an incorporated county in either a state or territory inhabited by paler folk.

Fair being fair, and Longarm having been in other parts of the west by now, he had to allow Pawhuska was downright civilized next to, say, the seat of Lincoln County, New Mexico, or, hell, Tucson, if one wanted to talk about surly redskins.

Most of the public buildings in Pawhuska were whitewashed, that being the B.I.A.'s notion of the way wood siding ought to look, even if white was a somewhat sinister medicine color to most Indians west of the Mississippi. Those private dwellings in Pawhuska not painted almost any other color than white had been left to turn a soft, silvery gray in the dry winds and sunshine out this way. Some cottonwood and willow still grew along the Bird, even within city limits, but most of the ground had been cleared and, Indians feeling about lawns the way they felt about a heap of other Wasichu notions, the silvery-gray to skull-white structures rose from packed earth red as the streaks down an Osage warrior's cheeks in the Shining Times. Red was another powerful medicine color. Not as unlucky as white, though.

Despite the size and civilized appearance of Pawhuska, Longarm and the Osage girl didn't attract near the attention they might have rolling into a white settlement just after suppertime with a buckboard filled with dead men. They'd had no tarp to spare for Green River Roy. So it hardly looked as if they'd brought taters to town with two saddle broncs trailing after. Martha looked as if butter wouldn't melt in her mouth as they forded the shallow river and drove up to the cluster of buildings around the flag-topped sort of glorified army barracks that housed the Osage agency and tribal council, when it was in session. The only government building still open at that hour was the combined police station and jail, of course, so that was where Longarm reined in.

When nobody came out, he told Martha to stay put while he paid a courtesy call on her law. She said she'd rather go try on some hats. So Longarm entered alone to find a couple of blue-uniformed Osage playing checkers. When he told them who he was and what he was doing there, the older moon-faced one looked pained, got to his feet, and held out a paw, saying, "I'll look, but I can't promise anything. I'd be Jerry Littlechief, if you want to put it in your report or something."

Longarm said he'd write them all up for an assist if they assisted him worth mention. The older Osage murmured something to the younger one in their own lingo. As his deputy broke out a coal-oil lantern for them, Longarm told Littlechief, "I met another Osage peace officer called Tallchief just inside your boundary line the other day. Are we talking titles or family names?"

The husky Osage shrugged and said, "Both, most likely. In the Shining Times we didn't *have* family names. You'd ID a man as, let's say, the Little Chief who leads the Dog

Society or maybe Many Ponies who's uncle happens to be the man called Bleeding Eyes.''

The younger Osage got the oil lamp's wick about as bright as it figured to get, and his superior nodded and said, ''*Heya.* Let's go see what dead Wasichu look like. It's been so long, I've sort of forgotten.''

As they all filed out, Littlechief continued for Longarm's edification, ''Since we came in and the B.I.A. gave us allotment numbers and asked us to make the same signs every time we drew money or supplies, we have taken to having everyone in the same family use the same name, usually just some ancestor's name—in English, of course. Those of us who remember still understand how real people should be named. You wouldn't. So let's not worry about it.''

Longarm started to say he knew more than some infernal redskins might think. But he bit his tongue. He wasn't being paid to show off how much he knew. There were no doubt army officers, and even Indian agents, who'd find him foolish for giving a rat's fart about the customs of a despised and hopefully vanishing race. So instead of saying he knew Indians were given a pet name at birth by their parents, a more official name by their peers as they grew up to take their place within the band, and a secret name only they and their spirits were to know as their *real* name, he just said, ''The one I had no tarp for, there, allowed his pals called him Green River Roy. Our customs ain't all that different once you study on 'em. We've just been making our signs on tax rolls, voting registers, and such a mite longer. Someday your several-times grandchildren will have no more notion why they sign in as Littlechief than I have who in thunder was first called Long way back in the old country. All I can say is that I'm sure glad my long-lost ancestor wasn't called something like Coward or Crook, both of which appear in the Denver City Directory.''

Littlechief suppressed a yawn as he took the lamp from his deputy and dangled it over the dead face of Green River

Roy, growling, "I've never seen this ugly cuss before. Let's have a gander at the others."

Longarm rolled aboard the buckboard to do the honors as he observed, "Old Roy, here, admitted he was trailing me lonesome, for a fee I find downright insulting. These other three told your Martha Tipisota they were seeking the one called Ben, who seemed to have been trying to hide out. How come Martha's allotment name mentions a white house? Isn't white the medicine color of Owl?"

Littlechief shot him a thoughtful look and said, "You *have* been paying attention, haven't you? It was her grandfather they first called the One Who's Been to the White House. Do you really want our whole damned tribal history?"

Longarm laughed and finished unwrapping the one called Larch as he replied, "Not hardly. I've enough to worry about right here."

Littlechief stared soberly down at the dead man's face as he decided, "Not as much trouble as this old boy got into, messing about where he had no business messing. Have you any notion as to why wicked Wasichu boys get the notion they can do most anything they want to here in the Nation? I've been to Kansas. More than once. It ain't all that different, or tamer, far as I could see."

Longarm agreed. "Dodge City of a Saturday night has to be at least as wild as any Indian Nation town I've seen so far. To begin with, it costs less to get drunk in Dodge."

"We don't allow no hard liquor at all in Pawhuska," the Osage lawman said stiffly.

Longarm managed not to smile as he answered, "Be that as it may, the question before the house is the identification of all these drunks from other parts, if at all possible, and their proper planting in the cold, cold ground in either event."

Littlechief nodded and opined, "I noticed the three you shot last night have already started to mildew a mite. You palefaces sure do turn funny colors after you've been dead a spell. It's small wonder you have more delicate feelings about dead bodies. If it wasn't for the picky, picky B.I.A., we'd still be allowed to dispose of the dead the easy way. But being we have to even bury our own these days, I reckon we can get Harry Threefeathers to display 'em out front of his hardware shop until no later than noon tomorrow, and then plant 'em over to the Moorish Cemetery. Harry'll charge you extra if you want 'em buried in *boxes*, though.''

Longarm established the going rate for a fine pine coffin crafted by Harry Threefeathers and decided four dollars a box sounded fair before he cautiously added he found it a mite surprising that the Moorish Congregation of the Indian Nation could be large enough to rate its own burial ground. The Osage lawman explained, ''We don't have any Moors among us aboveground, as far as I know. The plot we bury Moors in got started during the Jayhawking days when a palefaced Moorish gent rid down on a shot-up pony, shot up even worse, his ownself, to die on us after some days and nights of moaning and mortification.''

Longarm frowned thoughtfully and decided, ''Well, if the ex-mistress of the Mad King of Bavaria could wind up doing her spider dance for the edification of San Francisco, I reckon at least one Moor could have been mixed up in all that guerrilla fighting in bleeding Kansas. Might he have been left over from that U.S. Army Camel Corps they tried to start, just before the war?''

Littlechief shrugged and said, ''He never said. He just raved pure nonsense, or mayhaps Moorish, as he lay dying. We figured out what he was after. Papers among his effects identified him as a Moor called Haji Tim Stevens of the Mystic Shrine of the Alhambra.''

Longarm laughed incredulously and said, ''Hold on, I suspect you boys planted a Shriner, or a Mason, of that particular persuasion.''

Littlechief frowned and insisted, ''Miss O'Banion, the Wasichu librarian the B.I.A. picked out for us themselves, said the Alhambra was a famous Moorish palace in the

Moorish parts of some Wasichu old country.''

Longarm dryly observed that they had an Alhambra even closer, open around the clock, up in Dodge. He started to explain the ways a properly raised librarian named O'Banion could have been just a mite ignorant of Masonic matters, but Littlechief cut in with, ''It's not wise to dwell on the names of the dead, and Miss O'Banion died of the ague many summers ago. Her spirit would not be pleased if it heard you saying she had been a stupid person. It doesn't matter where that first Moor came from or how he wound up buried in our Moorish Cemetery. The point is that we bury anyone there who is not a Christian with kith and kin in these parts, see?''

Longarm said he did now, and after they'd jawed on some more about all four Moors in the buckboard, Littlechief decided, ''Hear me. We are speaking in circles, and the night is not getting any younger. I'll have my boys keep an eye on things here, if you like, while you take care of any other business you might have in town. You won't find Pawhuska wide open all night, like Dodge and other big, wicked cities. So unless you want to find everyone in bed by the time you can get to them . . .''

Longarm said, ''I'm thinking. I got to wire Billy Vail a progress report, talk to that Threefeathers gent you mentioned about the four cadavers, and then I still got to figure out where me and all this livestock means to spend the night.''

Littlechief stared absently up, the way Martha had last been seen, as he dryly observed, ''That's what I just said. It's none of my beeswax where man or beast beds down, as long as nobody presses charges. But Harry Threefeathers has a fine-looking woman and turns in early whilst the Western Union's open all night, so . . .''

Longarm thanked the Osage lawman for his helpful advice and proved he meant it by taking it. Harry Threefeathers was a pleasant, middle-aged cuss who, once they'd dickered some on price, agreed to store the four cadavers in his root

90

cellar overnight, put 'em on display on the shady side of his shop betwixt dawn and high noon, and see they were planted properly afterwards if nobody came forward to take corpse one off Longarm's hands.

Longarm knew he was likely to get stuck with the hundred-dollar grand tab. But if he did have to pay out of his own pocket, he'd have to admit he was being treated fair. Some small-town undertakers demanded as much as seventy-five just to bury *one* useless outlaw.

The Justice Department, having no use at all for a *dead* one, had a nasty habit of sticking federal lawmen with the funeral costs, if any. Longarm felt, and fortunately Billy Vail tended to agree, that such penny-wise and pound-foolish policies had no doubt led to many an unsolved mystery they'd never get off the books. For given the choice of reporting you'd gotten your man, dead, and thus lost out on the modest bonus for bringing him in alive, and finding yourself stuck with his damned funeral expenses as well, what kind of a choice was that for a lawman with a dead outlaw and a heap of wide-open country to work with?

After making his deal to dispose of these particular cadavers less informal, Longarm shook with both Harry Three-feathers and the town law, agreeing they'd all get to study on it some more in the morning.

Then, knowing Martha would notice her own buckboard farther off than anything else in such tricky light, Longarm drove it with all the stock down to the Western Union office.

The black-and-yellow sign out front was lit inside like a jack-o'-lantern. The counter inside was lit up way brighter, with a couple of hanging coal-oil lamps. But there was nobody in sight on the far side of the counter.

This became less mysterious when he heard a loud, metallic *whump* and the whole frame building tingled about him. To the casual ear it might have sounded as if they were doing some heavy repair work in the back. But Longarm didn't have casual ears. So when a gruff voice called, ''Check the front whilst you're about it, Provo,'' it was already too late. Longarm was down on one knee, six-gun in hand, as he heard another voice call out, "There's nobody at either door at this hour, you nervous nelly."

Longarm couldn't make out the exact answer to that. But the one who'd moved closer answered, "*You* stand out here and pretend to be the durned old clerk, then, if you're so smart. The infernal front door's locked. Any damn-fool Injun aiming to send a telegram at this hour will just figure the place is closed, see?"

Longarm shot a curious glance at the spring latch of the solid front door, wondering how he'd ever been so sneaky without trying. He was still wondering when the one called Provo snorted in disgust and said, "Of course it's locked. I locked it. But, shit, I'll lock it some more if you'll get off my back and open that infernal safe, Nick!"

Then Longarm heard boot heels clunking his way, casually but way too sudden, as he tried to determine which end, if any, this counter he was hunkered down behind swung open!

It didn't. The one called Provo simply rolled across it on his rump to come down on Longarm's side with the grace of two empty boots hitting a whorehouse floor. He froze like a fly in amber when he saw what he'd almost landed on top of. For Longarm had a finger to his lips as well as that .44 muzzle, almost touching the bulging crotch of the outlaw's saddle-worn jeans. The startled owl-hoot rider's own gun was still holstered. He was enough of a professional to grab for some roof rafters without being asked as Longarm rose, running the muzzle of his six-gun up the center seams of Provo's jeans and old army shirt. When someone called out from the back, the one Longarm had the drop on was smart enough to call back, "I told you it was locked." So the ones in the back got back to work, making enough noise for the one called Provo to smile uncertainly at Longarm and whisper, "Give me a break. I've never hurt nobody, and it's Nitro Nick in the back you really want, see?"

Longarm muttered, "Turn around and face the front windows. How many back yonder, and where's the clerk?''

Provo hesitated, sighed, and said, ''The clerk ain't hurt bad. He's tied in a corner, to your left as you come in. Nitro Nick is the only real crook on the premises. Him and my kid brother, Jude, are at the infernal Mosler safe to your right, and if I get Jude out here for you, could we mayhaps deal?''

Longarm pistol-whipped the helpsome cuss unconscious and lowered him gently to the floor to repose on his face with his holster empty and his hands cuffed behind him for now.

Then Longarm only had to roll over the counter, himself, and stomp his own less ferocious boot heels in the same ferocious way as he strode bolder than he really felt to join the boys in the back room.

It made Longarm nervous enough. It scared the two yeggs working on the battered, but still substantial, safe so badly that one of them let out a ripping fart and began to bawl like the mean little kid he still was at heart. The older and more sardonic-looking cuss with the hammer in one hand and cold chisel in the other stared up at Longarm, pale as a frog's belly, but managed a world-weary smile as he let go the safecracking tools and raised his dirty hands, asking, ''Who tipped you off, Lawman?''

Longarm risked a quick glance the other way, saw the telegraph clerk staring hopefully as well as bound and gagged, and told the well-known Nitro Nick to listen tight as he explained exactly what he wanted the old pro to do next. So Nitro Nick unbuckled his own gun rig with his left hand, let it fall wherever it had a mind to, and moved over to untie the Western Union gent as Longarm made the youth called Jude disarm himself and go stand in the corner.

A lesser lawman than Longarm might have told Jude to shut up when he asked about his big brother in that whiny voice. Longarm was smart enough to reply, ''Don't worry about old Provo. How did you boys think I got in here so quiet?''

93

It was Nitro Nick, the one who was supposed to be so savvy, who snarled and spat, "I knew it! That's what I get for taking the word of a fucking squaw man on the honor of two thieves! What did you and Provo ever thieve afore, Jude, penny candy outten your uncle's trading post?"

Longarm told Nitro Nick just to keep untying that poor Western Union cuss. Once the telegrapher had the wool sock out of his mouth, he yelled, "I want all these sons of bitches hung! Look what they done to me, and look at the gawd-awsome mess they've made of company property back here!"

Longarm said soothingly, "Don't cuss him, and don't swing at him afore he has you untied entire, pard. You don't look raped or murdered, and old Nick, here, should have known better than to use the usual soup on this fine new Mosler patent. I figured right off you had yourself a Mosler when I heard the soup go off and the safe door stayed shut."

Nitro Nick crawfished back as he slipped the final knot tying the telegrapher's wrists. But the feisty Western Union clerk came up so sudden, swinging, he split Nitro Nick's lip before Longarm could fire a warning shot into the floorboards, freezing everyone in place, he hoped, as he snapped, "That's enough. I mean it."

So the telegraph clerk said he wouldn't hit Nitro Nick no more, and Longarm said, "*Bueno*. The poor shit's got enough on his plate. At least twenty more at hard, federal."

The middle-aged safecracker stared saucer-eyed at Longarm to protest, "You can't be serious! You only got us on attempted. You caught us afore we could even get the box open!"

Longarm nodded and said, "Mosler patented that new door there, with assholes like you in mind. You must have been doing time for that other dumb job in K.C. when the papers ran the story, Nitro Nick. You see, they knew yeggs like you had learned to run a seal of beeswax, soap, or whatever down the crack of a safe door so's you could inject a stream of nitroglycerin the length of the door with dire results to the same, once you hit it a good lick with, say, a nine-pound sledge.''

The telegrapher gasped and pointed a finger at Nitro Nick, saying, "By Jimmy, that's just what they just done. That's the very hammer, over in that corner by the lunch buckets and such they breezed in with. Only, like you said, nothing happened when they whumped the door, save for all that chipped paint and them serious dents, I mean.''

A familiar voice called in from the front, "Who's back there, and why is Provo Woodson out here on his fool face with handcuffs on?''

Longarm called back, "I been expecting you, Littlechief. This time I got three *live* ones for you.''

As the Indian lawman and some others came on back to join the fun, Longarm continued explaining to the telegrapher in the time left. He said, "All Mosler done to get around the trick was simple but efficient. They just drilled holes inside the door frame, where they don't show from outside. When the yegg injects his soup at the top, it just runs out the bottom, collecting in some cedar shavings so's it'll never go off. The whump we all got to hear was way less soup than it takes to really damage anything delicate as a half-ton door made of boilerplate and cast copper. They fill the space betwixt the inner and outer steel with molten copper, because once it cools and sets, it's even harder to burn through or crack open than solid steel, see?''

Jerry Littlechief had entered, gun drawn, just in time to hear the last about cracking safes. He knew the telegrapher, of course. So all Longarm had to tell him was which one of the prisoners might be the one and original Nitro Nick and which one just seemed to be a pistol punk.

Indian lawmen were just as smart as white lawmen when it came to hearing folk out before they expressed any opinions of their own. So Longarm was only mildly annoyed when the Osage said, "We got the flier warning the world he chose as his oyster that Nitro Nick was loose again. Provo and Jude Woodson are both assholes too. But this is

95

the first time they've pulled anything worth hard time in Leavenworth, bless their little hearts.''

From the corner Longarm had stood him in, Jude Woodson bleated, ''Hold on! Who said anything about Leavenworth in connection with a little harmless fun here?''

Longarm smiled pleasantly at Nitro Nick as he replied, ''I know all three of you are slick as whistles. That's no doubt what inspired you to attempt armed robbery on an officious Indian Reserve, policed by the federal government, which has been known to dole out twenty years at hard for screwing a sheep.''

He pointed his six-gun at the battered safe as he added, ''Had this telegraph office been, say, in Coffeyville I'd have no jurisdiction as a federal officer, and you'd likely catch no more than two-to-five off Kansas. But being you're so *smart*—''

''Hold on, we're Indians,'' Jude Woodson insisted.

Jerry Littlechief snorted in disgust, and Nitro Nick snarled and said, ''Shut up, Jude. Can't you see the white one's too tricky by half? He already tried to trick us into thinking your brother peached on us when all the time the poor boy lay half dead out front!''

But Jude Woodson snarled back. ''*You're* the one who said mean things about old Provo, *white boy!* Me and Provo rates a tribal trial, and you just get outten this as best you can, hear?''

Longarm and Jerry Littlechief exchanged glances. It was sort of surprising how gents with so few other things in common could agree once both packed federal badges. By now the place was getting mighty crowded. So the Osage lawman told his Osage deputies to take all three Wasichu sons of bitches over to the Pawhuska lockup for now.

It was only after they'd been frog-marched away that Longarm dryly observed, ''I tricked a boy posing as Lakota by asking him in all innocence if he was a Hidasta, knowing most of us Wasichu refers to the same as Crow.''

The Osage chuckled and decided, ''You might as well

have asked a real Lakota right out if he slept most regular with his mother or his sister. I didn't have to trick those Wasichu brothers to know they're no more Indian than I could be Bulgarian. They're still going to try, though, and if their uncle gets just one or two easygoing drunks on the Osage Council to ignore their big blue eyes—"

"Hold on, Jude did say something about an uncle, and way before that Tom Tallchief made mention of an Indian trader called Woodson. Might we by any chance be talking about the same gent?"

Littlechief grimaced and replied, "Calling Gus Woodson a gent would be as accurate as calling a skunk a sweet little pussy. Other than that, you got the son of a bitch right. Runs the trading post at Gray Horse, mayhaps an easy day's ride from here. Some say he runs moonshine, dirty books, and other forbidden pleasures in from Wakan-Tonka knows where."

The Western Union man chimed in, "I know who we're jawing about. There being no telegraph office in Gray Horse, he uses our services here, now and gain. Can't say I ever took him for an Osage, though, no offense."

Jerry Littlechief said, "None taken. He's paler-faced than Longarm here. Got in with the Osage Council by marrying up with the eldest and ugliest niece of old Seth Stonepony. The two boys my boys just carried over to the lockup would be kin his own folk sent our way to live down some trouble they got into in other parts."

Longarm smiled thinly and said, "It didn't work." Then he turned to the Western Union man he'd rescued and said, "I've sure got a heap of messages to put on the wire, if you're rested up enough now."

The telegrapher said he not only felt swell but had a bottle of Maryland rye in the safe those rascals had failed to get into, thanks to Longarm and the Lord. Longarm said he liked Maryland rye just swell, and when Littlechief allowed he'd never tried it, the Western Union man got it out before they went back in the front to send wires all over creation.

97

Jerry Littlechief was pleased to learn that Nitro Nick had been out just long enough to rate a modest amount of bounty money posted on his otherwise worthless head. The telegrapher said he felt sure Western Union's insurance company could do even better by whoever wound up with credit for the capture. Longarm pointed at his fellow lawman of a darker hue and said, "Make sure you tell 'em old Jerry and his boys locked up the rascals in the end. I have neither the desire nor the time to attend many meetings of the Osage Council. Nitro Nick is bound for Leavenworth no matter what, and local fools who rob Western Union offices in towns where they're well known have piss-poor futures whether they can prove they're red, white, or blue. Meanwhile I was never sent here to pester anyone called Woodson. I may or may not be riding Gus Woodson's purloined horse these days, but that's *his* problem. For I rode into your strip with a clear conscience in pursuit of Frank and Jesse James."

He moved over to the counter and ripped off a yellow telegram blank to start writing a message to Vail from the wrong side of the elbow-high countertop as the telegrapher handed the bottle to Littlechief. The front door opened again, to admit one small, ragged-ass barefoot boy with cheeks of tan indeed. He asked which one of them might be Deputy Long from Denver, and when Longarm pled guilty, the kid said Miss Martha Tipisota had said to tell him he'd find her, the horses, and her buckboard at her cousin's place on Slippery Elm Street. When Longarm asked what the house number might be, the kid looked as if he might be fixing to cry. Jerry Littlechief told him to scat and added for Longarm's edification, "I know the house. Just a couple of dooryards up from the river, with blackjack oaks to either side of the gate. Miss Martha always bunks with Miss Wynona Widington when she's in town."

Longarm was more interested in the door the kid had slammed after him and said so. The telegrapher nodded and said, "I was hoping the Woodson boys had missed that as

98

I lay in the back, hoping someone just like you might come along.''

Longarm said, "I'd be more inclined to lock a door personal, than I'd be to simply guess.''

The clerk chuckled and replied, "Oh, Provo locked it, like he said. Only the lock's been busted for a month of Sundays and, being we're open twenty-four hours day . . . oops!''

Neither Longarm nor Littlechief asked why when the Western Union man loped back to take down a message coming in despite the hour. It only served to illustrate why even a small branch office such as this one stayed open for business around the clock.

Longarm finished his progress report to Billy Vail while Jerry Littlechief finished the bottle of Maryland rye. That might have been a more serious breach of B.I.A. regulations and the Federal Indian Code if the bottle had been less depleted to begin with, or if the good-humored but rugged Osage hadn't been able to handle his liquor better than many a Wasichu Witco.

Longarm had finished his chore by the time the Western Union man rejoined them with a bemused expression and the message he'd just transcribed. He said, "It's for you, Deputy Long, and speaking of small worlds . . .''

Longarm took the message to read instead of speculating about it. The telegrapher's block printing wasn't near as neat as his own, but as he read it over he saw he'd gotten it right the first time, loco as it read. He turned to Jerry Littlechief and asked, "Do you reckon old Gus Woodson and all the other little Woodsons will turn up for that hearing as to just how Indian those safecracking nephews of his might be?''

The Osage nodded and said, "Sure. I just told you both them boys had been placed in Woodson's care by blood kin. Is there something about them in that tellygram you're holding?''

Longarm answered bleakly, "Not exactly. My boss out

99

in Denver just passed on a tip from a paid informant in Louisville. Seems at least one of the James brothers has been playing farmer in Kentucky since the Northfield raid busted the gang up so good. I don't think even Billy Vail knew how scary this wire might read when he sent it this evening. He meant it to inform me I was likely wasting my time here in the Indian Nation.''

Jerry Littlechief nodded sagely and said, ''I can see how dumb it would be to look for Frank or Jesse here after hearing they're way off in Kentucky.''

Longarm shook his head and said, ''That's not exactly how the tip could be taken. One or more of the James brothers was seen in Kentucky, some time ago. What's more important is that we just learned the name one or both of the James brothers have been going by since the Northfield raid. It's *Woodson*, and we already knew they had blood kin in this here Osage Strip!''

Chapter 12

Marshal Billy Vail had been known to loudly disapprove of his senior deputy's detours down the primrose path, and Longarm did try to behave himself, within reason, while on duty. So until he'd been jolted by Billy's disturbing wire, he'd been planning to quit while he was ahead with the pretty, but sort of murderous, Martha Tipisota. It might have made more sense to just ride on by moonlight, once he'd made sure Cole Younger's Aunt Adeline was nowhere near Pawhuska. But knowing a heap of folk named Woodson would be swarming like flies around warm horseshit anytime now, he changed the cards on the table considerably. So once he'd left the Western Union, alone, he went swarming on over to Slippery Elm Street, figuring to at least get his infernal pony and possibles back, even if she was mad at him.

She wasn't. But it took a few minutes to make sure, since it wasn't her as came to the door, even after he'd figured out which one went with the familiar buckboard parked betwixt two damned cottages with oak-infested dooryards.

Considering her name and address, Wynona Widington didn't look all that Osage as she stood in her doorway smiling up at him with the lamplight from inside shining through her summer-weight cotton skirts. Her face wasn't bad, either. But what made it hardest of all to buy her as a Wynona was that bodacious mop of strawberry hair piled up atop her fine-boned head. It made her look as wild as any Indian, and the way she'd bound her bun in rawhide-strung trade beads should have been even more convincing. But it wasn't. She wore her war paint, a lot of it, like a white gal as well. He couldn't tell, just standing in her doorway, how much of that stink-pretty was stuck to her sweet hide, and how much she was burning Chinese style, inside the house. She told him to come on in and that she and Martha had been worried about him. So he tried not to worry as he stepped into her front parlor and let her shut the door behind him, knowing just how that fly in that poem must have felt, even though this particular spider was down-right lovely, once you got to see her better with the lamplight aimed the other way.

He took off his Stetson and placed it atop an upright piano by the big and sensuously soft sofa she herded him toward. When she suggested he get rid of his old .44-40, frock coat, and vest while he was at it, he wasn't sure just how he ought to answer. He was saved from having to try when the more familiar, as well as more Indian-looking, Martha came in, stark naked from her black stockings up, to trill, "It's about time you got here, you mean thing. We were about to start without you!"

Longarm felt his ears getting red as he tried to brazen it out with a raised eyebrow and thin smile. The one he'd never even kissed yet had the innate modesty to turn a mite strawberry all over as she murmured something about coffee and cake before turning to dash off somewhere. As soon as they were alone, Longarm told Martha they'd embarrassed her cousin. Martha simply answered, "Don't be silly. I told her you did it real sweet-natured for a Wasichu hung so well, and *she* hasn't had any, either, since the last time the herds were in town."

He said she hadn't struck him as that desperate a gal, and as they stood there a spell, he fully dressed but her naked

102

body doing most of the sweating, Martha decided, "You may be right. Don't you just hate a tease who talks a great love life and then goes all goose-bumped and crossy-thighed when she's offered a nice, no-strings screwing?"

He laughed and confided, "I'm sure glad you see our, ah, friendship that way, honey. For since last we got friendly, the case I'm working on has gotten more complicated, and there's just no telling when I may or may not have to simply light out, mayhaps without time to even say *adios*."

She nodded soberly and said, "We know about you catching those Woodson brothers and some outsider in the act. Speaking of getting caught in the act, do you mean to stay outside me indefinite, or shall we get down to some nice dirty fun in the guest room, damn it?"

He had to allow that the front parlor seemed an even dumber place to start. But as she led him by the hand through a beaded archway into a cozy corner room almost overflowing with a big four-poster, he felt obliged to whisper something decent about their vanished hostess, adding, "I'd feel better starting without a permit from the lady of the house if there was an infernal door lock, or even a door."

Martha said, "Pooh, let her just stay behind her own beaded curtain if she don't want to know what's going on in here."

Then she had Longarm down on the bed, and he wasn't sure he wanted anyone to know what was going on as the pretty little spitfire got to work on his fly buttons, giggling about how she meant to kiss it and make it well.

He told her to let him get undressed, too, so's they could go about it right. As he sat up to strip, she helped him, asking with childlike innocence how anything a man and woman could do to each other at times like these could be right or wrong.

He didn't answer. He was afraid she'd laugh at him if he told her he felt bashful about strange gals catching him in unusual positions. By this time Martha was so worked up, she didn't give a damn what position they started in, as long as they got started right away. So it came to pass that when Wynona Widington did come in to join them, carrying a tea tray piled with coffee and cake, she saw Martha on her hands and knees across the mattress, with Longarm standing bare-assed and barefoot behind her, a big hand gripping each tawny hip, to service her barnyard deep and dirty.

He stopped—red-faced, of course. But he'd have felt even dumber hauling it out so hard. So he just gulped and muttered "Howdy" as Martha arched her spine and groaned through gritted teeth, "More! More! Don't stop *now*, you brute!"

He murmured, "Uh, Miss Wynona just come in with some cake and coffee for us."

But Martha pleaded, "I don't care about other folk coming with anything. I want to come with you up my ring-dang-do, you son of a bitch!"

As Wynona placed the tray on the lamp table by the bed, Longarm smiled sheepishly at her, across Martha's upthrust rump, to ask, "Does she always talk so dirty when she's a mite excited, ma'am?"

Wynona moved over to stand beside him as she calmly replied, "All us girls talk much the same when we're excited."

Then she shucked her summer shift as casually and as quickly as if it was a corn husk and dropped to her own hands and knees beside her darker cousin, arching her own spine to present as glorious a view of receptive maidenhood, in this case strawberry blond between somewhat bigger and softer, as well as whiter, buttocks.

As he stood behind his volunteer and somewhat mismatched team, as hot to trot as they were, Longarm could only exclaim, "Decisions . . . decisions" and throw it even faster to old Martha, since any other course would have been downright nasty in the state he had her in by this time. The idea of her whiter cousin in the very same position beside her got the lusty young widow even more excited, and as she moaned in sheer delight and fell forward off Longarm's turgid shaft, he almost wound up ejaculating in midair. But good old Wynona was there to catch him with her own love maw as he thrust it into her to the roots, hissing ''Jeezuss!''

She shoved back against his less powerful but politely repeated thrusts, purring, ''Ooh, I felt that. Don't that first deep thrust feel grand, even when you *ain't* coming?''

Just to her left, Martha had rolled on her back, tawny legs spread and lush lower lip in a pout as she protested up at them, ''Don't just *talk* about coming. *Do* it so's *I* can have a turn at bat again!''

Wynona giggled and said she didn't have any bats on the premises but that there were all sorts of mops or broom handles if Martha just couldn't wait. Martha giggled, too, and while she didn't go that far to keep up with her cousin, Longarm found it oddly inspiring to watch one pretty little thing fingering her fool self, while he was humping another one for her, watching for inspiration. Old Martha came that way more than once, to hear her tell it, before he was back between her tawny thighs to make her come again while Wynona watched them, moaning, ''Oooh, that looks so wicked!'' playing with her at the same time.

But nothing good or bad can last forever. So he said so, wistfully, as they inhaled cake and coffee afterward, in hopes of getting their second wind—or his, at least. When Longarm observed that it hardly seemed fair that a critter as weak-spined as a man was expected to do all the work, Wynona said, with no shame at all, ''I know. Two boys and a girl can get into way more interesting positions, and the one time I turned in with *three* boys all at once . . . well, that was almost more than I could take.''

But she'd taken it, as Longarm found out in more detail than he cared to, once Martha got to questioning her more wordly, as well as whiter-looking, cousin from the big city. Longarm tried to tell himself it was nice to know he wouldn't

105

be leaving any brokenhearted Osage maidens weeping in his wake when the time came to ride on. He still wished women didn't have to brag so about the other dongs they'd taken in the damnedest places, once they got to bragging at all. For as he'd discovered before, to his considerable chagrin, Longarm found the fantasy of three in a boat less fun in real life than it promised to be, just dreaming such doings-up lonesome.

Longarm washed down the marble cake he'd been chewing and said, "I'd just love to lay you both at once if I was built less awkward, gals. But if we're to go on like so, even in my own dull way, I'd best confess we have to study on how safe it might be for the both of you."

Wynona said, "Pooh, we both know how to take care of ourselves."

And Martha confided, "I don't have to bother. After I'd been wed a spell with no more results than a good time had by all, I asked the B.I.A. surgeon how come, and he said I couldn't get in a family way if I tried and . . . Speaking of trying, Custis . . ."

He laughed and quickly explained, "The night is young and I'm so human. Hold the wicked thought. I'm talking about one or more of you getting *shot*, not knocked up."

That inspired Wynona to demand the names of any other gals he might have been trying to knock up on or about the Osage Strip. He assured her he had all the gals he could handle present and accounted for before he explained, "I'm expecting trouble with a well-connected Indian trader called Gus Woodson. I'd been warned about him even before I got a tip that the James brothers have been known to evoke his family name. I can't see any of the Osage Police I've met so far in cahoots with the James and Younger gang. On the other hand, if Gus Woodson has pull with the Osage Council, and they simply order their own lawmen to stay out of it and let the fool whites work it out as best they can—"

Martha cut in with, "That's silly. I've seen that loudmouthed old Wasichu here in town a time or two. He comes to your armpits, standing on his toes.''

Longarm shrugged his bare shoulders and said, ''The Continental Congress declared all men equal in 1776, and Sam Colt made sure they were in 1836. Flat-footed or on tiptoes, Gus Woodson may have more than one bone to pick with me, and I hear he runs in bunches.''

Martha insisted, ''You and Jerry Littlechief just locked up the only Woodson boys big enough to matter. All the old fool's Osage kids are too bitty to fight anybody big as me and Wynona, here.''

Wynona, who dwelt a day's ride closer to Gray Horse, sounded less certain as she decided, ''The paleface is mighty thick with other Wasichu from other parts, for the son-in-law of old Seth Stonepony. What about that blinky-eyed Woodson, who had words with young Frank Dalton that time? He wasn't too little to fight, and he should have been ashamed of himself for picking on that Dalton boy so.''

Longarm blinked himself all the way awake and got rid of his cup and saucer as he demanded, ''Hold on, honey lamb, you're the first one I've talked to in this town who's admitted to even knowing the Daltons as well as the Woodsons by name!''

Wynona lay back invitingly on his left side as she answered, simply, ''That's doubtless on account that neither the Woodsons nor the Daltons live here in Pawhuska. Gus Woodson's licensed trading post is way over by Gray Horse, like everyone's already told you. Lew Dalton doesn't have any permit from the B.I.A. so he sort of trades as best he can, over the tailgate of his covered Conestoga, see?''

Longarm said, ''I know about selling moonshine on the fly. Might either of you know where the Daltons bed down when they ain't trying to get arrested?''

Martha, on his right, yawned sleepily and opined, ''Nobody's going to arrest nobody for selling liquor in the Indian Nation, unless they try to sell bad stuff. Present company excepted, you Wasichu sure make up stupid laws. I'll allow

107

some Indians can't hold their liquor. I got a Cheyenne breed planted under my compost heap to prove that. But if you really want things all that peaceable, why don't you pass a law forbidding *everyone* to drink?''

Longarm grimaced and decided, ''Mayhaps some day they will. I've yet to meet a politician with a lick of sense about human nature. But for now we've got enough bootleggers to worry about right here in your Indian Nation. You ladies knowing it better than me, how do you reckon the wandering Daltons pick up the letters they seem to get now and again from Cole Younger, over Missouri way?''

Martha didn't know. Wynona said, ''They could pick up all the mail they wanted at the post office here in Pawhuska, as long as it was sent to them in care of General Delivery, Pawhuska, I.N.''

So he blessed her, kissed her, and then had to kiss Martha some more after he'd finished with Wynona. He decided not to ask if either knew how come the Daltons and the Woodsons seemed to be at feud. For at the rate he was evoking answers from such friendly gals, he feared he'd be too weak to face either a Dalton or a Woodson when the time came.

Chapter 13

That Scots poet had been on the money about the best-laid
plans of mice and men. For though he got to lay both the
gals he'd shacked up with, before *and* after breakfast, Longarm soon learned just how much pull Gus Woodson had
when he ambled over to the Pawhuska lockup to see whether
Provo or Jude Woodson wanted to talk about their blinky-
eyed kinsman and the Dalton boy.

Neither brother was there. The deputy pulling desk duty
out front said they'd been remanded to the custody of their
legal guardians, red and white, but that they still had that
stupid Wasichu safecracker locked up in the back, if Longarm wanted to talk to him.

When Longarm said he'd rather talk to Jerry Littlechief,
the Osage filling in for him looked uncomfortable and declared, "Oh, he had to ride over to Coffeyville and see
about turning Nitro Nick over to Kansas. Wakan-Tonka
knows when he'll be back."

Longarm dryly observed that he'd noticed they had no
telegraphic communications with the outside world, here in
this big tipi ring. He added, "I'd best have a word with
your Seth Stonepony, or somebody as big on your council.
For this is raw as steaming shit in a collection plate, and I
defy even Stonepony to say it ain't!"

The Indian lawman looked as if he'd have agreed with Longarm, had he been able. But he could only look away and murmur, "Ain't nobody on the council bigger than Seth Stonepony. He's the deacon of our Wasichu church, as well as the dream singer of the Kit Fox Lodge. I can't say what he'd say about steaming shit, if somebody asked him. Nobody can right now. He's rid off into the hills, seeking a vision, he says."

Longarm nodded grimly and replied, "I'm getting some mighty clear visions without stirring a foot from town. Which way did those two safecrackers stir, back to Gray Horse?"

The Osage, who'd have had the bastards locked up in the back if Longarm had had any say in the matter, looked pained and said, "They do say their uncle, Gus Woodson, trades out of Gray Horse when he's not out peddling from his wagon. I'm not sure we ought to call either Jude and Elmo safecrackers, though. The way the writ we got from the council was worded, they were just sort of watching when that purely white rascal, Nitro Nick, set out to blow that safe and, let's face it, *failed*."

Longarm said he got the picture and spun on one heel to get out of there before he started another Indian War the War Department might not want him to.

He considered asking the clerk at the Western Union how such a big Wasichu-owned company felt about helping him make up some charges he might have left out the night before.

He decided not to waste his time. Western Union had at least as much political clout as the Osage Nation. So, seeing they were as political as most such outfits, they'd have already gone along with the cover-up in exchange for the head of Nitro Nick and continued good relations with the powerful Seth Stonepony and his desperately ugly daughter. As he paused to light a cheroot Longarm wondered what the real Pocohontas Rolfe née Powhatan had looked like. He'd always wondered about that story ever since they'd

110

told him old John Smith had palmed the princess who'd saved him onto another Englishman.

As he headed for Wynona's place instead, he told himself, he even tried to warn himself, that he and Billy Vail combined were just a mite smaller than Western Union's legal department. But what the hell, he'd been meaning to question Gus Woodson in any case, and now he had a fine excuse.

He didn't want to upset either gal. So he was saddling Sapatonka up, out back, when the strawberry roan Wynona caught him at it in her bitty stable. He didn't ask what she was doing out back in her kimono. When he told her where he had to go and why, she pleaded with him to wait right there till she got back from the smaller shed with the half-moon cut in its door. Then she ran for it, without waiting for an answer either way. So he felt some remorse but no real shame as he muttered to the Tennessee walker, "We'd best get going, lest you get shocked silly by bawdy behavior in that very pile of hay, you poor, nutless unfortunate."

He led the pony out front, as quietly as possible, soothing it with a dirty description of that scandalsome freak-show gal who'd taken on that burro that time, to prove it could be done.

Sapatonka didn't seem interested. Longarm swung himself up into the saddle out front and got to ride off a ways before he heard a shrill female voice demanding he return at once, damn his eyes. But he just rode on, not looking back, as he mentally checked off all the possibles fastened to his good old McClellan saddle.

You could fasten a heap without galling your mount, because for all his faults as a general, General George McClellan had been a swell quartermaster.

Maybe too good and too kindhearted for leading the Army of the Potomac in the Peninsular Campaign against the more lethally inclined Robert E.

No troops on either side had ever been as well fed, well armed, or gussied up than McClellan's spiffy boys in blue.

Then, at a place called Antietam, poor McClellan met up with ruffians in butternut gray who just didn't give a shit for spit and polish, and the next thing anyone knew, you could walk clean across the torn-up fields from the Dunker Church to the Bloody Lane on dead bodies, both blue and gray, without ever putting foot one to the ground.

As they rounded a corner, safe at last from any flying lead or china Wynona might peg after them, Longarm patted the big black's neck and confided, "McClellan won at Antietam, only the poor asshole was too thunder-ghasted by the carnage all around to notice that. The Army of Virginia had taken even heavier casualties, and Lee was in full retreat, only shooting back as usual as he ran for it. Had old George McClellan ordered the fresh troops he still had in reserve to go for broke as Lee limped off . . . well, he never did, and that's how come the war lasted three more years. But you got to admit old George designed us a swell saddle and, what the hell, once they put old Butcher Grant in command, he had himself a big, well-armed, and fully equipped army to grind poor Robert E. down to size with."

By this time, Pawhuska being less a metropolis by white than by even civilized tribal standards, they were approaching the city limits, whether the Bird River was still within rifle range or not. They were naturally headed west, since that was the way one got to Gray Horse, and Gray Horse was where they thought they were headed.

Then Longarm heard hoofbeats and the sound of someone calling his name. The voice was male and Longarm turned in the saddle to see yet another Osage deputy chasing after him.

As they both reined in atop a rise the Indian said, "Martin Kruger said you might want to know. So he sent me after you."

Longarm frowned and decided, "Right, Martin Kruger would be the oddly named Osage that Jerry Littlechief answers to when he ain't answering to Seth Stonepony. So

112

what does the council think I ought to know that I didn't know before?''

The Indian said, "Honest, old Martin just found out. Young Frank Dalton met up with Pukwanna Kruger over to Okesa.''

Longarm said, "I know where Okesa is. Keep going.'' So the Osage did, saying, "They met friendly, sharing a smoke out front of the general store. So Frank Dalton was likely telling the truth when he said he'd hired on as a top hand at the Rogers spread, over to the east near Vinita.''

Longarm pursed his lips and consulted his mental map of the Indian Nation before he decided, "I got most of the bigger settlements set right within a day's ride. So we're talking a Cherokee outfit in the Cherokee Strip, right?''

The Osage answered, "Sore of. Vinita's up a side creek of the Neosho in the Cherokee Strip, true enough. But the Rogers are Wasichu. Mostly Wasichu, leastways. You know you got to claim *some* Indian blood to hold land anywheres in the Nation.''

Longarm grimaced and said, "A battered old bawd called Belle Starr explained all that to me the last time I passed through Younger's Bend, a good hundred miles south of Vinita.''

Then he stared through, instead of at, the other rider as he mused, half to himself, "Now that's sort of odd, as soon as one studies on it. Did Frank Dalton say what his folk might or might not be doing up at the north end of the Cherokee Strip?''

The Osage shrugged and replied, "I wasn't there. I'm telling you about the conversation secondhand, or is it third?''

Longarm didn't think it mattered, either. He reached for a smoke to give himself more time to think, and sure enough, the Indian asked if he wanted a police escort at least as far as the Osage-Cherokee line. When Longarm asked how come they'd suddenly gotten so concerned about his health, the Osage lawman answered innocently, "Well, you did arrive with a buckboard full of dead outlaws, and both the Woodson boys promised, in parting, to clean your plow if ever they laid eyes on you in or about Gray Horse.''

Longarm thumbed a match head alight and held it cupped in both hands as he lit his cheroot despite the west wind across the rise before he replied, ''I started out for Gray Horse just now. Locating me a Dalton in the other direction entire calls for reconsideration. I wasn't sent here to pester safecrackers the Osage Council smiles upon. I was sent to see if the Daltons have any notion where Frank and Jesse might be and, if so, whether they'd like to share such family secrets in the higher cause of justice and the considerable bounty on those otherwise useless sons of bitches.''

The Osage sent to change his travel plans said, ''I can tell you no Wasichu outlaws worth that much are hiding out among *my* people. The Cherokee Council ain't half as strict about such matters as our own, though.''

Longarm was too polite, or too smart, to pass any remarks about the two the Osage had just turned loose that morning. He just heeled Sapatonka back toward town and made small talk with the pesky Osage clean across the Bird River until, way up the east slope, seeing Longarm was safely on his way and not at all desirous of a posse riding with him, the Indian recalled his old woman was serving grits and gravy with turnip greens come noon, and seeing Longarm didn't want to come home with him for some, they parted friendly.

As the Osage lawman turned back, Longarm rode on to the east at the same casual pace, aware more than one pair of eyes were likely to be watching his back from the town back yonder. He topped a gentle rise and held his mount to the same course and pace so they'd show on the higher rise to the east as expected.

Assuming they were dumb enough, that was.

Knowing he enjoyed a certain rep for having brains, Longarm rode farther than most riders would have before he reined Sapatonka to a halt where the trail ran shady through tanglewoods, saying, ''They'll expect us to cut

114

around to the north, closer to the Kansas line, if we cut around at all. I'd best have a peek at the real map before we go sneaking around to the south, where the land's laid out more busted up.''

Sapatonka didn't offer any objection. The tall, dark walking horse had discovered some fresh green sprouts of what the Osage called bow wood, and everyone else called Osage orange. The stuff was really a sort of ornery relation of the mulberry bush. Stock smart enough to avoid its sharp spines seemed to enjoy the leaves. Longarm had yet to see man or beast bite into the so-called oranges the trees dropped in the fall. For though they looked a lot like green oranges, they were hard and likely as tasty as billiard balls.

The army survey map he took out of a saddlebag warned him not to circle to the south of Pawhuska if he wanted to wind up in Gray Horse. It wasn't simply that the contour lines were closer together that way, indicating bumpier range. By some perverse Osage logic the more steeply eroded range to the south, patchworked by open grazing and woods marked ''impassable'' by hopefully lazy survey crews, was more thickly populated. That meant that even if he could get through, he was way more likely to be spotted, and spotted by folk more likely to report a mysterious Wasichu to the Osage police than anyone else Longarm wanted tagging along.

He refolded the map and put it away before he dismounted a moment to rest his pony and water a cottonwood that looked as if it could use the liquid better. Then he remounted, hauled Sapatonka's nose out of the sticker bush, and heeled the brute south-southwest through the tanglewoods, assuring it, aloud, ''I ain't really lost, and we won't know whether I'm refusing to obey orders until such time as we find out where the Daltons really are these days.''

Sapatonka didn't answer. Longarm ducked under the gnarled limb of a wind-tipped blackjack oak that had stretched smack across the deer trail they seemed to be following as he continued. ''I know that Indian told us the eldest Dalton boy was punching cows in the Cherokee Strip. The Osage are considered a civilized tribe these days, so they have the same constitutional rights to fibbing as the rest of us. Ain't it odd how nobody back there seemed to know a thing about the Daltons before I mentioned calling on other white trash Frank and Jesse might know in these parts?''

Chapter 14

Longarm crossed the Bird River six or eight miles down-stream from Pawhuska, and it still looked more like a creek than any river to a gent who'd grown most of the way up in West-by-God-Virginia. He'd been west of the Big Muddy long enough by now to accept the more casual ways they named things out this way. Names bestowed by the first half-civilized folk clapping eyes on some natural feature tended to stick. So a heap depended on who and when.

The Grand Tetons or Big Tit Mountains might have been named a mite less bawdily if they hadn't been spotted first by French Canadian fur traders, or if the government survey man who'd taken their word on what said peaks were called had spoken French. Things got named buttes or chimneys, canyons or gorges, arroyos or gullies, according to the lingo of the first vaquero or buckaroo who'd reined to whistle and remark, "Hot damn, look at that whatever!"

The more serious Western weather accounted for the odd ways streambeds could be named. Depending on how re-cently and how hard it had been raining, near or far, one got to cross and recall a river, a creek, a dry wash, or, hell, just a draw that didn't deserve its own name. The Bird River would have rated as a mighty shallow creek if it had been up to Longarm to discover and name it that afternoon. It had doubtless been in flood after a gully-washer the day someone else had named it.

Longarm had often been chided for his ruminations on such matters. But as few but old Billy Vail seemed to savvy, a lawman never knew when some nit nobody else felt up to picking might hatch into a full-blown conviction. Hence, even as he rode up the grassy slope west of the Bird, he glanced back, muttering, "Denver's Cherry Creek would be the Cherry River if they'd come upon it during the Flood of '64."

Then he almost reined in but didn't, as he spied another rider, just busting out of the trees atop the *east* slope of the wider draw the Bird had carved for elbow room in wetter times.

Another rider in cattle country, even cattle country owned by Indians, seemed reasonable enough. The way the distant figure on the buckskin pony crawfished back into the line of trees didn't.

Longarm hadn't reined in for a farewell glance at the creek they'd just forded, so it was simply a matter of swinging into a more sensible position in his own saddle as he told Sapatonka, "Well, we tried. The trouble with civilizing Indians is that it makes it harder to lie to 'em. Let's just mosey on, innocent, till we can see our way to test that Osage rascal's tribal tracking lore."

He rode on up and through the first timber growing along the next rise to the west. Betwixt the shade and steady winds sweeping over the rise, there was scant underbrush between the hardwood trunks and, thanks to the distance from any settlement, a lot of it was virgin growth. So Longarm loped Sapatonka down the far side, across stirrup-high cowslips and blue-eyed grass, grunting, "Needs some good old ornery tanglewood if we're to really test that pesky tagalong. A schoolmarm, a white one, could track steel-shod hooves across virgin forest duff."

Knowing they were under observation, without having to look back again, Longarm rode up the next open slope at an angle farther south, chuckling to himself as he told the black walker, ''Aside from being easier on your long legs, this ought to make him wonder some if he was told we're headed for Gray Horse instead of, say, the Arkansas crossing at Prue Town.''

He rode farther before he added with a thoughtful scowl, ''Now that's mighty odd as soon as you study on it, Sapatonka. It ain't been *that* long since the Osage was hunting buffalo instead of punching cows. They still do a heap of hunting in such swell deer range, unless they just hate venison. So how come that fool Osage on the buckskin is trailing us like a stray dog from the big city sniffing after a bitch in heat? If he knows about where we're headed, why ain't he trying to get there first, the way even bitty kids with slingshots head off rats around a city dump?''

His mount offered no suggestions, but Longarm still had it figured by the time they'd made it over the next rise into a really messed up patch of tanglewood. He grinned wolfishly and growled aloud, ''If he was riding for the Osage Council, he'd *know* where we were headed for the simple reason that they don't *want* us headed there. So he can't be riding for them. Who's left?''

First things coming first, he reined south-southeast through the hellish tangle of intertwined hardwood that had sprung from the stumps of earlier clear cutting as perversely as the serpentine locks of that Medusa gal in the illustrated book of Greek bedtime tales he'd stumbled over in the Denver Library that time. It was tough going, even after Longarm dismounted to lead on foot, holding the reins in one hand and twisting the arms of trees with the other. For it took a tough tree to grow this close to longitude 100° to begin with, and only desperadoes of the vegetable kingdom make it back up as second growth by sprouting from the stumps and bulling up through the litter left by the trash loggers, who messed even with virgin peckerwoods.

Most of the stubborn shit was cottonwood, which at least stayed busted once you busted it. Buggy whips sprung up

119

from chestnut stumps was way tougher to bust, and shagbark wouldn't bust at all. They had to go around most of the blackjack oak as well, but one way or the other Longarm got them so deep in the tanglewood, they could see out the other side. The first thing he noticed on the mostly open, sunny slope to the west was a couple rutting wild and carefree behind a haystack. That was to say, the haystack was between them and the sod house, the outbuildings closer to the bottom of the slope. The Indian boy and white or blond breed gal going at it hot and heavy in the hay must have thought nobody ever came in from the east through all the tangled timber. For if they had, they'd have doubtless had at least their socks on.

Longarm backed Sapatonka to where the walker could nibble some cottonwood leaves, tethered it securely, and said soothing, "I can't watch folk screwing and that rascal trailing us and you at the same time. So behave your fool self here, and I'll be back when I've more to report to you, hear?"

The black walker got to munching joyfully as Longarm moved back for another peek at the happy couple behind the haystack. There was a chestnut stump about the dimensions of a milking stool, save for the buggy-whip shoots sprouting skyward all around the flat seat where solid wood met still living bark. Longarm chuckled as he got out his pocketknife, muttering, "I swear they must have known the day they cut you down, old tree, that someday you'd make a grandstand seat for a Peeping Tom. With the right whittling a man could turn you into a sort of Windsor chair with a regular backrest and all, right?"

Then he got to work, and thus it came to pass that less than half an hour later Boulder Bill Beaumont, a vaguely sinister young man with no visible means of support and a Harrington & Richardson .44 slung low spied the dark mass of Longarm's browsing mount among the fluttering leaves and tangled saplings ahead. So he slung himself sort of low as well, drawing his six-gun and staying put as he tried for

120

Longarm's lesser outline in the dappled green confusion. After what had happened to the other boys Boulder Bill wasn't about to get any closer to that deadly deputy without knowing for sure where he was and, more important, which way he might be facing. Boulder Bill had heard it was dirty to back-shoot other gents. But what the hell, they hung you just as high for shooting lawmen front or back, and they weren't paying him enough for this job to even consider suicide.

Then Boulder Bill heard a distant voice calling out for its dog, its woman, or whatever. The hired gun followed the muzzle of his .44 in that direction. When he got close enough to the far side to spy the bare-assed couple hunkered, quiet as church mice behind the haystack while a fat old gent in bib overalls yelled in all directions from that barnyard down below, Boulder Bill grinned sly as a fox and twice as mean. But they hadn't sent him all the way to the Indian Nation to go sloppy seconds after no Indian, pretty as that little farm gal might be as she lay there shivering.

Boulder Bill stopped breathing as, tearing his eyes from the white gal's tempting flesh, he spied tobacco smoke spiraling up through the leaves way closer, and then, son of a bitch if, tracing down, he didn't spy that familiar dark Stetson with the Colorado crush and that bitty spangle of sunlight flickering back and forth on that tobacco-brown tweed Longarm wore. So yonder the big rascal was, seated on a stump to watch the show, and it was too bad, in a way, that the big bastard would get to go with his last moment of vision the sight of a pretty naked lady. But at least the son of a bitch would be dead at last. So what were they waiting for?

Boulder Bill had left his own saddle gun aboard the buckskin he'd tethered on the far side of this tanglewood, not knowing it was possible to haul a horse through it. But his double-action H&R had a five-inch barrel and, not considering himself dumb enough to get into quick-draw situa-

121

tions, Boulder Bill had left the factory-adjusted sights the hell alone.

He still braced his gun hand's wrist in the fork of a shagbark hickory as he carefully drew a bead on the shadowy outline of the intended target. He sighted first on the clearly visible crown of Longarm's hat. Then, knowing the dire results a high-carrying shot could lead to once you'd aimed at the back of a man's fool *head,* he lowered his sights until he decided by guess and by God that his first round had to hit just below, just above, but in either case close enough to the big bastard's heart. So all he had left to do was take three deep breaths, let the last one half out, and pull the damned trigger.

He pulled it a second time, by agonized reflex. So there were three shots in all before Boulder Bill wound up staring up at Longarm's gently smiling face in confused horror.

For aside from the bonfire burning inside his rib cage, as far as Boulder Bill could figure out, he hung sort of half crucified down Longarm's side of the shagbark, his one wrist now caught in the fork above his head. It hadn't seemed that high before his legs had somehow turned to empty wet socks. They were wet, he knew numbly, because he no longer had any control of his bladder, either. He tried to get his numb feet under him to rise, discovered neither would move, and stared reproachfully at the man standing taller as he calmly reloaded his own .44-40. Boulder Bill croaked, "I can't get my arms or legs to work. Did you back-shoot me just now, you sneaky cuss?"

Longarm nodded amiably and said, "I had to. Couldn't shoot you at all before I let you display some murderous intent. They don't allow me to shoot others just for acting nosy. So, knowing you were trailing me and seeing a handy way to determine why, I sat a sort of scarecrow for you to treat any way you wanted. I left one of my cheroots a-smolder on a flat stump you can't see from here. You ought to be able to figure things out from there. So now we're going to talk about *you,* Boulder Bill."

The spine-shot killer would have blanched if he hadn't already lost too much blood to get any paler. He asked, "What was that you just called me? I generally go by the name of Smith."

Longarm nodded and said, "I've long admired your cough drops. But you sure do resemble another pillar of the community called Boulder Bill Beaumont, and by any name, you'll smell about as sweet in a day or so unless we arrange a proper funeral for you, old son."

The spine-shot killer had been bled by now to that dis-interested state when even the naturally fearful could get to wondering why they'd always felt so scared before. Long-arm had watched other men die in war and peace. So he wasn't too surprised when this one shrugged the one shoul-der he could still move and said, "I don't much care what you do with me, once I can't feel it. Get six pretty maids to keen over my coffin or shove a ham bone up my ass and let the dogs carry me away, for all I care."

Longarm said, "I can't promise all six maids will be pretty. But you have my word on at least a pine coffin. Might even manage cypress, lead-lined, if you'd tell us where to send the bill."

Boulder Bill stared heavy-lidded at nothing much, saying, "Ain't got no kin as value me that highly. Never get caught in bed with your brother's woman if you plan on going home for Christmas in times to come."

Longarm nodded soberly and said, "The dying young of your brother is a matter of public record, you sweet-natured cuss. I was talking about the party or more who hired you to send *me* to an early grave as well."

Boulder Bill chuckled dryly and said, "I don't owe any lawman toad squat. But tell me something, Longarm, is it true you federal deputies ain't allowed to just ride off and leave us rot, even if you have to pay for proper burials out of your own pocket?"

Longarm was saved from having to answer that just yet by the sound of crashing and thrashing branches and a gruff

123

voice bellowing, "Come back and face the music like a man, you Muskogee son-of-a-bitching bastard!"

Longarm called back, "Don't neither of you fire this way, no matter what you're fussing about!"

The gruff one called back, "Who says so?" and so Longarm called back, "I say so, in the name of the federal law!" and then, as he spied that Indian farmhand from the haystack crawling this way through the brush, mighty pale-faced, Longarm waved him closer and added, "I'd be U.S. Deputy Custis Long, and I'm standing over a dying prisoner here. So come on in polite, if you're coming."

The young Indian got there first, blanched at the sight of the dangling, half-dead Boulder Bill, and wheezed, "Old Man Mathers is after me with a pitchfork for some reason! I suspicion he's gone mad and thinks he's that spirit you call Satan!"

Longarm said, "Crawl over yonder and shut up, then. I was just talking about the hereafter with this other gent."

He tried to, leastways. But when he asked the second time without getting an answer, he stepped closer to feel the side of the killer's throat and mutter, "Shit, I killed him before he got to tell me who sent him to kill me."

Then he turned as the old cuss in bib overalls busted through the walls of greenery, pitchfork and all. The sight of Longarm with a six-gun gripped in one hand and a dead man's throat in the other gave the elderly nester pause indeed, until he spied the young red-skin cowering on the far side of Longarm and roared, "There he is, the half-breed ingrate who defiled my lawfully wedded woman after we'd given him room and board as if he *belonged* in these parts!"

Longarm let go of the dead outlaw and holstered his side arm as he smiled uncertainly and said, "Forgive me, pard. But unless I've rid off the map entire we have to be just about smack in the center of the Indian Nation, Mister, ah, Mathers?"

The old-timer with the pitchfork nodded to retort, "Damned A. Pure Osage on my maternal grandmother's side, which is more than this two-faced half-nigger *Creek* can say!''

The kneeling object of the old man's rage protested, ''I'm pure Muskogee, German and Irish, damn your eyes, and Miss Daisy June told me she was pure Swede and dangled Saxon.''

''Did that give you any right to trifle with her?'' the outraged Mathers roared, trying to get around Longarm with the pitchfork.

Longarm blocked his way, saying, ''Hold on, now. I ain't certain this is any of my beeswax, for I'll be switched with snakes if I can see how federal law fits in, but I just don't see how I can let you pitchfork anyone around here without you offer me just cause. So why don't you start at the beginning?''

Mathers growled, ''Lord knows when it begun. They told me I was taking a chance, sending off to K.C. for a mail-order bride. But it seemed to be working out just fine until, oh, say fifteen minutes ago. I'd took me a nap right after my Daisy June served me Swedish meatballs and, ah, other swell things. I usually sleep until around three, since I hired that two-faced Muskogee there, to do some of the heavier chores.''

Longarm said that sounded reasonable. Mathers scowled at his young hired hand and continued. ''Today I woke up early, from an awful dream about this young rascal and my Daisy June. I run outside and called and called, only nobody answered. Then I heard your gunshots, and when I peered up this way, I seen Bobby there, hightailing it up into these here woods with his jeans in one hand and his shirt in the other. So now that I've caught up with the disgusting little shit, I'll thank you to stand aside and let me fix him so's he'll never trifle with my Daisy June again!''

Longarm nodded agreeably but said, ''We'd all deserve to be pitchforked if dream sinning counted. I mind the night I met up with Miss Sarah Bernhardt and Marie Antoinette over in France and . . . well, suffice it to say, we get to do

125

things in dreams as ain't possible in real life."

Mathers insisted, "They was going at it possible enough in the hayloft out back when I woke up. The only thing different about my dream and real life was that I flushed this horny hired hand outten a haystack instead of a hayloft just now."

Longarm shifted his weight awkwardly and said, "I saw this old boy behind that haystack long before you did. Don't see how you could have seen him sinning half as good as me, and even this dead rascal here. You say you caught him in the act with your woman?"

Mathers looked away and confessed, "I was chasing him too hard to notice what *she* might have been doing behind that haystack."

"Then you can't say she was there at all," Longarm insisted.

To which the outraged husband replied as insistently, "Hell, she must have been, likely hiding deep in the hay like a shamed ground squirrel, now that you've got me to thinking back on it. For what else would even a lazy farmhand be doing jay-naked in a haystack at this time of day?"

Longarm shot a not unkind glance at the breed he'd noticed bouncing on the blonde and said, "I hate to tell on a fellow sinner, even to save his life. But you can see it's for the greater good if I say what I seen you going at so hot and bothered behind that haystack, can't you?"

The Muskogee gulped and begged him not to.

To avoid both their eyes, Longarm started going through the pockets of the dangling dead man as he insisted, "I know just how you feel, old son. I'd feel mortified if anyone caught me acting so silly in broad-ass daylight too. But surely you can see it's the only way I can hope to save a marriage and mayhap your life as well."

The Muskogee protested, "You got no right to horn into my private life, damn your peepsome eyes! What you seen me doing might be sort of frowned on in the Good Book, but if every man who ever done it got arrested for it . . ."

126

"He's right," Longarm confided to old Mathers with a wink, adding, "When that Muhammad gent was dictating his own scriptures, someone asked him why he didn't say word one in his Koran about jerking off. He told 'em nine outten ten men jerked off, and the tenth one was a liar, so why not let Allah decide. That's what them Arabs call the Lord, Allah."

Old Mathers stared at his farmhand in dawning delight as the latter's brown face flushed redder than it had any right to. As Longarm pocketed the silver certificates he found in Boulder Bill's billfold and idly examined the unconvincing ID, the old nester grinned like a shit-eating hound and jeered, "So *that's* what you was up to behind my haystack! Whacking your Creek cock whilst you was supposed to be slopping the hogs or weeding my Daisy June's herb garth?"

The red-faced hired hand stared down at the leaf litter between them as he stammered, "The h-hogs had been slopped, and Miss Daisy June had told me to just let her herbs be afore anyone went anywheres near that infernal haystack."

"Couldn't wait till nightfall, eh?" the older man said jeeringly, adding for Longarm's edification, "If you'd seen my Daisy June just now, you'd know why this young mutt jerks off over her ever' chance he gets."

Longarm said, "I'm sure I would. This more important pest I just had to shoot IDs his fool self as a William Smith with the library card and voter registration card you can pick up for the asking in most any trail town."

Mathers didn't seem to care about the recent past of the late Boulder Bill. He demanded, "Was he really stripped down to the very buff, just to play with his own horny hard-on?"

Longarm said, "Well, as I viewed the scene from some distance I failed to see any ladies giving him a hand job, and I don't recall him wearing his shirt or jeans, come to study on it. The way you get 'em to register you as a voter

127

in a strange town is simple. You ask at the barbershop which party runs the local machine. Then you just have to drop by the right party's headquarters and say you'd like to vote for their slate, if only you could.''

He put the billfold back in Boulder Bill's sucker pocket as he continued. ''Once you're registered as local Democrat, Republican, Granger, or whatever, you got enough ID to demand a library card or, hell, join the local Klavern if the county law's still Klan.''

He straightened back up, observing, ''You don't want to Klan-up in any state or territory that backed the Union, of course. You boys would know if they had any Indian Klaverns, of course?''

Neither seemed to know what he was talking about. He shrugged and said, ''I reckon Indians, even breeds, would find it hard to join a white-supremacist outfit, even though most of the civilized tribes come out for the South.''

''Not mine,'' said the Muskogee. So naturally the older man who claimed Osage blood called him a nigger-loving Creek as well as a jerk-off artist.

Longarm said soothingly, ''All that trouble betwixt the North and the South was thrashed out years ago, and I don't even want to talk about which side *I* might have rid for. My present problem is the disposal of this dead body. It wouldn't be decent to just ride off and leave him dangling like that.''

Old Mathers suggested, ''You shot him. This cut-over stonesome ridge ain't been claimed by anyone yet. You want to borrow a pick and shovel, pilgrim? Hiram, run down to the toolshed and fetch this Wasichu lawman a pick and shovel.''

The embarrassed Muskogee sprang to his own feet, as if more than willing to oblige. But Longarm said, ''Hold on, I promised this boy at least a pine box and his own little plot of hallowed ground.''

He cast a thoughtful glance at the dangling dead man, noticed how sneery Boulder Bill's pale face still struck him,

128

and decided, "A numbered plot in some public potters' field, leastways. My boss can be so picky about such details in my reports."

Old Mather asked if there was any bounty on the rascal, brought in smoked and salted. Longarm was tempted but decided he'd twisted the truth enough in this neck of the woods. So he turned to the hired hand with a curious smile as he answered, "No law saying anyone around here can't *try*. But I feel somehow certain that Hiram, here, would be willing to haul the cuss into the nearest settlement and ask any sky pilot who's willing to plant the poor wayfaring stranger right."

Old Mathers was way more surprised than Longarm when his hired hand allowed it seemed only his Christian duty, and even offered to shake on that.

Chapter 15

Longarm could have had possom or deer for supper. For when he tethered the black walker and buckskin cow pony he was traveling with now, he spied a fat old possom pretending to be a hornet's nest or something up in the blackjack oak next to the more tasty cottonwood he'd picked out for the ponies. The possom no doubt found the acorns all about it more to its own taste; nothing but mighty tough bugs browsed oak leaves.

Longarm wasn't hungry enough to browse on possom, and when he spied a deer moving out from the line of trees he'd picked for his own night camp, he felt content just to admire its cautious grace. You had to let venison hang a spell lest it give you the trots, and in any case, he didn't want to fire gun one in the gloaming, knowing how far a gunshot carried on the evening breeze.

There didn't seem to be anyone settled close to this wooded ridge, as there'd been during his shoot-out with the late Boulder Bill. But the only way to avoid visitors after dark for certain was by giving them no call to feel curious, no matter how far off the sons of bitches might be enjoying their own supper.

Enjoying was mayhaps too strong a word for the way Longarm felt about cold beans washed down with tomato preserves, but the cattle-drive standby that didn't call for a cook fire still tasted better than the cold grub he'd been served in wetter woods than these in the hills of Tennessee. His after-supper cheroot smelled a heap better than the tobacco some of the boys had found on the dead after Shiloh too. The only good thing to be said about the way an army fed you and sang you to sleep on a rainy night in the field was that once you'd been through that, you never bitched about cow camp or even Indian camp grub. So Longarm didn't. He turned in early without trying to brew coffee cold, and got an early start the next morning with the dew still on the range.

That was mostly burr grass and such tough-stemmed flowers as cows didn't admire much, away from the scattered patches of timber. But as he rode along he saw enough bluestem and even love grass to guess the Osage weren't overgrazing their strip too badly. From time to time he spied a cow, which lit out wild as any deer the moment it spied him, of course. The Osage were still raising pure Mex calicos or longhorn stock that could fend for itself against all comers and live on anything a goat could eat. That wasn't saying housewives back East could get their families to eat longhorn beef, now that wages were up and everyone was getting picky again. But the British Army was still serving lots of that bully beef they cooked tender in the can, so anything on four legs could be sold for *something* a head to the big packers like Armour and Swift.

As the day wore on, the carpet of grass all about got more worn and threadbare. The clear cutting of even second growth for firewood indicated more crowded conditions ahead as well. So when Longarm spied the smoke of more than one stove pipe rising off to the northwest, he consulted his survey map and told Sapatonka, ''If that ain't Gray Horse up ahead, at last, this map's wrong.''

Then he stopped in the first strip of cover they came to, in this case crack willows growing along a creek too pitiful to be on the map, and proceeded to swap saddles and bridles.

131

As he did so, he explained to Sapatonka, "I still love you. Only I'd be dumber than you if I rid into a strange settlement aboard a mount reported stolen there. So I'll just leave you here with plenty of shade and water whilst me and Buck, here, scout ahead a mite."

He fed both ponies some cracked corn and stuck a fresh cheroot in his own mouth before he mounted the buckskin, forded the bitty stream without wetting all four hooves, and rode on into the town of Gray Horse, which was really more like a few shacks clustered around a whitewashed post office, identified as such by a flagpole and an elderly white man whittling on the front steps.

Longarm reined in, dismounted, and tethered the buckskin to the flagpole before he strode over, braced one boot on a step, and said, "Howdy. I'd be U.S. Deputy Custis Long, and I'm looking for Gus Woodson, who runs the trading post here at Gray Horse."

The older man went on whittling willow with his barlow knife as he replied impassively, "You found him. I'm the postmaster, the justice of the peace, and, if push comes to shove, the chairman of the Gray Horse Democratic Committee. I understand you've been riding my horse, even afore you arrested my two nephews the other night, you infernal Republican."

Longarm smiled thinly down at the old cuss to reply, "President Hayes may be Republican. I've rid for the Justice Department under more than one administration, and since you brung it up, I find it sort of odd to meet such a staunch supporter of any party in these parts, since Indians don't have the vote any more than women do."

Old Woodson tossed what was left of the willow twig at the pile of shavings near his feet and put his barlow knife away as he sniffed and replied, "They vote for me in the tribal elections they're allowed to. I rid for the South, and it'll be a cold day in hell afore I lets even an Indian register Republican, hear?"

Longarm said, "I disremember which side I was on that

132

long ago. I knew the Civilized Tribes still had some few rights to self-government. Hadn't heard a Wasichu or, hell, a Lakota, got to run on any ticket or even own land in this here Indian Nation.''

Old Woodson cackled. "A lot you know. Indian is as Indian says, and my full-blood Osage wife says I'm Osage enough for her.''

"Is that how come you're holding your trading license as a white man?'' Longarm asked him, dryly but gently.

Woodson didn't get the sarcasm—or didn't want to get it, at least. He nodded innocently and said, "Damned A. I wasn't fibbing when I put my race down as white on my application. I never even told my Osage in-laws I was Indian by birth. They said that was jake with them, and I could be Indian by marriage if I wanted. It's all a matter of inter-pretation, and if you think you can arrest me for being a falsified Osage, you just try it. I'm as much an Indian as Colonel William F. Cody is a colonel, damn it!''

Longarm had to laugh before he allowed, "Even as Buf-falo Bill he never held a higher rank than army scout, ci-vilian. But it ain't my job to decide whether he's an officer or you're an Osage. So let's get down to what I *did* ride all this way to talk over with you.''

The old Indian trader got to his feet, saying, "I want my horse, and you can't have my nephews. But I'll buy you a drink whilst we thrash that out.''

The old geezer seemed headed for a low-roofed rambling pile just across the way, whether Longarm wanted to tag along or not. As the much taller and younger lawman fell in beside Woodson he asked if that was a saloon over yonder and, if so, how come.

Woodson growled. "I know you can't open a saloon on an Indian reserve. If you could, I'd have done so many moons ago, as my in-laws put it. Yonder's my trading post, more like a general store, since the Indians in these parts get their government allotments in cash. I ain't allowed to sell 'em the fine Cherokee corn squeezings I keeps for my

133

own medicinal purposes. Nobody squeezes corn better than the Cherokee. They larnt the art back in the Blue Ridges afore we fired the King of England and declared the Cherokee too childish to drink their own swell liquor.''

Longarm allowed he'd heard much the same moan from Mescalero Apache, who made better mescal than most Mexicans. He added that he was a deputy marshal, not a revenuer, as he followed the old grump inside. The place was dark and smelled midway betwixt a general store and saloon with a tang of tipi smoke thrown in. The potbelly stove was cold at this hour, but when you sniffed hard, you could tell it had recently been burning cow chips and corncobs. Longarm noticed the old-timer made no bones about keeping the quart jars of corn squeezings in plain view near the cash register, on the same shelf stocked with patent medicines the Bureau of Indian Affairs considered Heap Bad Medicine for its charges. Longarm knew Pinkham's potion for women's complaints was only about fifty proof, but had it been up to him, few white folk would have been able to buy that semilethal mix of opium and alcohol called laudanum without at least a note from a licensed sawbones. But he didn't comment as Gus Woodson poured them a couple of jiggers of joy juice.

He offered to clink. But the old trader just downed his own dose without ceremony and quickly poured another as he muttered, ''Nobody got more outten corn than old Martin Mankiller. There's some argument as to whether the Scots or the Irish invented the whiskey still, but since the Cherokee are half Scots-Irish, it hardly matters.''

Longarm tasted cautiously, admitted with his fingers crossed that the stuff seemed smooth, considering, and asked the old man if he'd ever had any liquor dealings with Lew Dalton.

Woodson wrinkled his nose and replied, ''I thought we'd just agreed the best moonshiners in the Nation are at least half Cherokee. I know Dalton. Might even be related to his white wife, way back on my mama's side. But me and Lew

134

are more like business rivals than kissing kin. We both sells medicinal alcohol—albeit only to white folk, you understand. Neither of us would be dumb enough to *make* the stuff our ownselves.''

Longarm finished enough of the shit he'd been served to be polite and put the half-filled jigger on the countertop between them as he asked, ''How come? You surely don't enjoy more than a two-hundred-percent markup on goods and services to your Indian tribe, right?''

Woodson said, ''Wrong. You can't skin Osage much more than you can skin anyone else since the smart-ass savages have been sending their kids to B.I.A. schools.''

He reached out to pat a pile of cotton flannel blankets at one end of the counter as he added in an injured tone, ''I've been trying and trying to unload these swell blankets for no more than twice what I paid the jobber, and them stuck-up Osage just won't buy 'em at any price. Them bright colors come from genuine German coal-tar dyes as neither run nor sun-fade, neither. So what else can anyone ask from an infernal blanket, damn it?''

Longarm knew. So he said. ''For openers it's sort of nice when blankets don't dissolve in hot, soapy water like paper. I know that brand of trade blankets of old, and it's always surprised me anyone would go to the trouble of spinning blanket yarn from cotton linters and paper pulp, but there you go.''

He added soothingly, ''It could be worse. You're right about the bright colors coming from genuine German dyes, and I once cracked a case involving wood pulp, dyed and flavored to be sold and fed to reservation folk as canned beef. The hell of it is, the Indians *ate* a heap of it afore I arrived on the scene.''

Woodson said defensively that he stocked no canned goods unfit for consumption by white folk, or at least their colored help. Longarm said he'd been admiring the brand names on the labels and asked if they could get back to Lew Dalton, explaining, ''I ain't interested in his Indian tradings.

135

I was sent to jaw with his wife about some of her kin and, come to study on it, you say *you* could be related to the Youngers on your own sweet mama's side?''

Gus Woodson shook his head firmly and said, ''Couple of Pinkertons got here way ahead of you on that, a year after Cole Younger and the other survivors of the Northfield raid got put away for the rest of their poor lives. I told them what I feels just as free as I tell you here and now. I hardly knows the Daltons, Lew or Adeline. He's no kin to nobody. Adeline might be distant kin to us Woodsons on her mammy's side. Nobody named Woodson ever rid with the James–Younger gang, and if it's true what the Pinkertons say about that pesky Jesse using the Woodsons' good name as his own on occasion, he's got even less right to it than Cole Younger. For poor Cousin Adeline ain't at all related to the Kentucky Baptist preacher, Robert James, as spawned the wicked Frank and Jesse. Me and Cousin Adeline might or might not be distant kin to Zerelda Cole James. She'd know better than me. The Pinks told me she still sends Christmas cards and such to Cole Younger in his prison cell. I wouldn't know the dishonest young cuss if I woke up in bed with him, and to and tell the pure truth, I wouldn't want to.''

Longarm was tempted to ask how Woodson's nephews, Provo and Jude, might be feeling since they got out of jail over to Pawhuska. But that would have been a dumb way to question a suspect. So he fished out two cheroots, offered one to Woodson, and told the old-timer as he struck a match for the both of them, ''I'd like to sort of climb Adeline Dalton's family tree with her my ownself, if you have their current address. I was just told they'd moved over to the Cherokee Strip. Might you know just where?''

Gus Woodson got the cheroot going better before he replied with a dubious frown, ''I heard the old pirate was running a roadhouse over near Kingfisher. Let's talk about my horse. Anyone can see you rid in here aboard a buckskin cow pony. But afore that you was riding all over creation,

136

or at least the Nation, on a black Tennessee Walker. I know you're going to have a hard time believing this, but I used to own me a black Tennessee Walker I liked a hell of a lot more than this two-for-a-nickel smoke, if you think it makes us even.''

Longarm assured him, ''If I've wound up with your horse under false pretenses, then the more fool me and I'll be proud to return it and bear the anguish to my own pocket. But let's just eat this apple one bite at a time. I was asking about where I might find Adeline Dalton, as I recall.''

Woodson answered flatly, ''I recalls asking about my horse. Afore I bites your damned apple or even finishes this smoke, I'm still missing me a solid black gelding, six years old and standing a tad over eighteen hands. The gent as sold him to me had no papers to prove it but said I was getting a Tennessee Walker, and I saw no reason to doubt him. Everyone who knows horseflesh knows what a Tennessee Walker looks like. Your turn, lawman.''

Longarm replied, ''The apparently honest horse trader I dealt with in Coffeyville tells a tale of a man in a hurry willing to unload a Tennessee Walker cheap. Let's start with your own sad story. You say you bought such a mount off a dealer who had *no papers* as went with such a bargain, Gus?''

The older man looked more sheepish than shrewd as he allowed, ''I don't offer bills of sale with the jars of medicinal spirits I may or may not sell, neither.''

Longarm nodded and replied, ''It would be rude to ask whether they were red or white too. Keeping things simple, was the gent in such a hurry to sell you a horse a white man or what?''

Woodson said, ''He looked white. I never ask. Blue eyes. Light brown hair. Said he was anxious to get on home after a horse-swapping tour out our way and—oh, yeah—he did say something about knowing Lew Dalton, if I wanted to check up on his honesty or lack thereof. I never did, of course. I just now recalled that much about the cuss.''

Longarm sighed and said, "You should have paid more attention to him. He looks much the same as the gent in a hurry to sell the same or mighty similar horse to Hank Hehaka in Coffeyville *after,* not *before,* the fine steed you'd bought off a similar-looking dealer wound up lost, strayed or . . . Do you have a name to go with such an ingenious horse thief?"

The dishonest old man's jaw dropped as Longarm's full import sank in. He said, "Hold on, now. The boy I dealt with said he was well knowed by all the Daltons in the Nation and, last I counted, there was dozens of the same."

Longarm nodded and said, "You just said Lew Dalton was no better than yourself, and I wouldn't expect you to double-check with a rival you can't locate on the map for me, either."

Gus Woodson growled, "I'll be switched with snakes if what you intimate so smug don't work! That slick-talking, blinky-eyed horse trader must have rid on home to Missouri aboard the very Tennessee Walker he'd just sold me a few days afore!"

Longarm dryly observed, "He told Hank Hehaka he was from Kentucky. I wouldn't be surprised to learn he has kin there as well. Did he have a name and, more important, was he missing the tip of the middle finger of his south paw?"

Woodson considered before he replied. "He answered to the name of Howard. Dingus Howard. Can't say I counted his fool fingers. Does it matter if he was missing one or more?"

Longarm nodded soberly and replied, "A man could call himself Howard as easily as he could call himself Smith or Jones. The Pinks say Jesse James has been reduced to solo horse theivery in his hopesomely declining years. You're not the first one out this way who's mentioned them blinky eyes our Jesse's afflicted with. Said infested eyes are blue. His hair's sandy brown. He stands five-eleven in his socks and a tad over six foot in his boots. He lost that fingertip cleaning a hairtrigger pistol in Bloody Bill Anderson's guerrilla camp, near the end of the war. They say he was more surprised than hurt when he blowed his own fingertip off. They say he just stared at the mess to pronounce it the dingus-dangest thang, and that's how come his brother and others he rid with during the war have called him Dingus, not Jesse, ever since.''

"Then Dingus Howard . . . ?'' Gus Woodson gasped, but Longarm quickly added, ''Frank James is known as Buck by close friends and relations. That don't mean every horse thief called Buck has to be Frank James. The slicker who seems to have flimflammed us both could be calling himself Gus Woodson or, hell, Custis Long right now. The only way we'll know for sure involves my catching up with him and that one mark of Cain the real Jesse can't hide. So do we have a deal or not?''

The old slicker asked just what sort of a deal Longarm had in mind. The more honest, as well as younger, man replied with a disgusted snort, ''We point each other the right way, damn it. Your stolen horse is way closer. So you can help me figure out where the damned Daltons may be as I show you where I left old Sapatonka tethered.''

That naturally inspired the original owner to ask who or what a Sapatonka might be as he circled back around the counter. Longarm made a mental note that the older man was ignorant of Osage or just stupid as he replied, ''Big Black seems a natural enough name for your missing mount to me. You say the Daltons might be over around Kingfisher these days?''

As they headed for the front entrance together Woodson explained, ''White nester settlement just north of Fort Reno and south of the Cimarron. Lew Dalton don't get along with Indians as good as me. So he gets to move more often. They'd know for sure, and have a better notion why, if you asked at the Pawnee Agency betwixt here and yonder. I don't know just why the Daltons got run outten Pawnee Town. Like I said, we ain't never been all that close.''

139

By this time they were out under the plank awning, and Longarm had every intention of leading the old fart down to the willows where he'd left Sapatonka, even though it was going to cost him. But while Longarm had been content to live and let live as far as local lawbreaking went, neither Provo nor Jude Woodson had known this when they'd heard the big deputy who'd arrested them in Pawhuska was here in Gray Horse to do . . . what?

So they were waiting out front, inspired by guilty consciences and corn liquor, to do whatever morons had to do when, to their added chagrin, Longarm seemed to be marching their poor old uncle out into the hot sun to Lord only knew what fate!

Old Gus Woodson yelled, ''No!'' just before he caught a wild shot aimed at Longarm with his own chubby chest. Longarm's aim was better, even starting later. But he still lost his hat to one of Provo's rounds as he slid sideways to one knee, firing back to fold Provo in the middle before putting one in Jude.

Longarm second shot had less stopping power, wherever in the guts he'd hit the asshole. But it didn't much matter whether a man went down or not, as long as he dropped his own gun to stagger off down the street, making noises like a she-wolf giving birth.

By the time Longarm had put his hat back on and rolled the dying Gus Woodson into a no more comfortable but mayhaps more dignified position, the dusty street was a heap more crowded, and Jude Woodson lay sprawled in the middle of it, making a heap less noise. A lean Osage wearing gun-barrel chaps and a federal badge came Longarm's way with his own gun out. He kept the muzzle aimed politely when Longarm flashed his own but still insisted, coming in, ''I hope you have some explanation for what just happened, Wasichu. I didn't think much of the younger Woodsons, neither. But old Gus, there, is related by marriage to Seth Stonepony!''

Longarm answered soothingly, ''I didn't gun him. They

did. After that things just happened sort of natural.''

The old-timer bleeding on the sun-bleached planks between them opened his eyes and muttered, ''That's the way it looked from here, Zeke. I don't know why the boys turnt on me like so. But I can't say I'm all that surprised. Neither one of the young snots has ever been worth spit in the main ocean. It's what I get for telling my sister I'd let her unruly brats board with me till the law out her way lost interest in 'em. Their father was no damned good, neither. We told her not to run off with no infernal Mormon, but would she listen?''

The Indian lawman cocked an eyebrow and demanded, ''Where were those boys wanted, aside from the other night in Pawhuska, I mean?''

Their uncle didn't answer. Longarm saw he couldn't, and gently shut the dead trader's eyelids as he softly replied, ''Utah, most likely. That ain't the only place the Latter-day Saints ever settled, but when you consider Provo, Utah, as well—''

''That don't work,'' the Osage protested, adding, ''If poor old Gus Woodson was their *mother's* brother, how come Woodson was their given name?''

When Longarm didn't answer, the Osage nodded half to himself and agreed. ''Gus just said the two of 'em were hiding out amongst us poor, ignorant savages. Do you reckon we could find out who wanted 'em, for what, if we wired Salt Lake City?''

Longarm shrugged and said, ''It's a free country, and a big territory when you consider the bastards are both dead, whatever they might have done in other parts under other names. You're going to want to make a full report of this shoot-out to your own tribal council, right?''

The Indian nodded soberly and said, ''The B.I.A. gets a carbon copy as well. But don't worry. I just heard the poor old Wasichu identify his killer or killers, and praise the Lord, neither you nor any Osage will have to stand trial for gunning Seth Stonepony's son-in-law!''

141

Longarm got to his feet, reaching for spare .44-40s to reload with as he replied, "I know a pony called Sapatonka who might be cheered by that almost as much as me. I have to get on down the road to the new settlement of Kingfisher now . . . ah, Zeke."

The Indian frowned and said, "Hold on. I still have to account for these other mortal remains to the council, and I hope you don't expect me to say *I* shot 'em!"

Longarm cast a thoughtful glance around, noting as he did so, and as he hoped Zeke might, that none of the curious brown faces watching at a still respectful distance had actually witnessed all that much.

He said, "Why not? You just now said Jude and Provo seemed to be wanted in other parts, and even if there's no bounty money on 'em, I doubt old Stonepony will be displeased with the lawman who avenged the death of his ugly daughter's only husband."

The lanky Osage grinned like a schoolboy spotting a ripe apple near a fence line as he turned to stare at the two dead villians. But it still took Longarm a smoke, a light, and a lot of jabber before the Indian agreed that that did seem to work out best for the both of them. So all in all, the morning was just about shot by the time Longarm was free to ride out to the southwest, mounted on the buckskin and leading the black Tennessee Walker. He figured this was no time to be changing horses. He had to be across the Osage line before anybody changed his mind.

Chapter 16

The Pawnee Reserve—it was too small to call a strip—
began an hour's ride and an Arkansas River out of Gray
Horse. The Arkansas was not a stream to be crossed just
anywhere, even in high summer. So the post road forded a
wider, but hence shallower, stretch at Ralston, as they'd
dubbed the cluster of unpainted frame buildings around the
post office cum general store on the Pawnee side of the
ford.

Like the Osage, the Pawnee were a Western nation added
to the original Civilized Tribes as a sort of afterthought once
Washington had seen how well Andrew Jackson's draconian
Indian Policy seemed to be working out. By the time most
of the Indian Nation had sided with the Confederacy during
the War Between the States, it had been too late to declare
anyone in pants a wild Indian again.

To be fair, the Pawnee had assimilated to white culture
about as well as anyone could have expected them to. In
their own Shining Times the Pawnee had been a Caddo-
speaking nation sort of midway between Osage and Cherokee or Sioux and Iroquoian in lingo and custom. Too ornery
to live at total peace and too smart to take on the U.S.
Army, the Pawnee had taken to scouting for the blue-sleeves
with an enthusiasm many of their neighbors, such as the

Osage, had never quite forgiven them for. That was likely why no Osage settlement faced Ralston across the brawling brown Arkansas. Longarm didn't care. He'd scouted for the army himself in his time, and Pawnee Bill, the showman giving Buffalo Bill a run for his money back East, seemed as decent and not half the drunk his rival was.

As he reined in out front of the general store he spied some ragged-ass kids playing baseball in the schoolyard across the way. Naturally the school was shut-down for the summer. Other than that, it looked much the same as any other, and while all the kids were doubtless listed as Pawnee by the B.I.A. more than one of 'em looked as white or whiter than some of the kids Longarm had shot it out with in his spitball days.

As he dismounted, a foul ball bounded across the dusty road at him and the two ponies. He hung on to the reins with one hand and scooped the ball up with the other to throw it back. As he watched the kids scramble for it, he gave himself a mental kick for taking this long to come up with such a simple notion. For this wasn't the first time he'd been sent to track down a man with a mess of kids; hardly anyone with a lick of sense had as many as fifteen.

Once inside, he assured the old white woman behind the counter of his good intentions by allowing he was in the market for a gunny of oats for his ponies and some canned goods and smokes for himself. As she was putting his order together on the counter between them, he added, "I see you have the back fixed up as a post office, and I've been keeping company with telegraph poles all the way from Pawhuska, ma'am. So might there be a telegraph office on or about the premises?"

The old woman sniffed and said, "Western Union must feel they're too grand for Ralston. Their nearest office would be in Pawnee Town, a dozen miles on down the road."

He thanked her sincerely, anyhow. It could have been worse. He did need the extra trail supplies, and she could have said there was no Western Union at all on the Pawnee

Reserve. He knew that if push came to shove, he could always shin up a pole and tap into the line with the old Army Signal Corps key he packed among his possibles. He decided to wait, though. Signal Corps style was a tedious way to send and receive even short messages, and the old bat had just told him Pawnee Town was no more than two or three hours off.

It was time to pay up now. So he proceeded to do so, asking her for a receipt at the same time. When she looked as if she might be fixing to cry, he explained he rode for the government and hoped to get his travel expenses back from them sometime before he died.

She sighed and said in that case she'd try, if he'd forgive her handwriting. He'd no sooner said it was the payroll clerk's misfortune and none of his own when she brightened and said, "Seeing as you're federal, you might be able to use the agency telegraph. Who am I making this bill out to, by the way?"

He placed his open billfold on the counter to save them both from having to spell Custis more than once as he allowed he hadn't noticed any B.I.A. buildings in town, save for the schoolhouse across the way.

She said, "There ain't none. That one sprawl serves as the town hall, the school, the medical clinic, and so forth. They was cutting down on needless expenses in the Nation, even before President Hayes got elected on his promise to tidy up President Grant's wasteful Indian Policy."

Longarm assured her he'd met other Indian agents doubling in brass since the big cleanup of '77. She suggested he go around the back and knock. Then she perked up even more and added, "Oh, unless your department's took to hiring Longs by the bushel, one of your fellow deputies was by the other day, looking for you by name. I naturally told him I'd never heard of you. How was I supposed to know you'd be coming in that very front door, long after he'd ridden on?"

Longarm smiled at her uncertainly and said, "We'd best

plow that furrow one more time—slower, ma'am. For openers, I didn't know I'd be here, myself, until earlier this very day. After that, things get even more mysterious. You say there's another white man, claiming to be a U.S. Deputy like me, who knows where I'm headed before I do?"

She handed him his receipt, along with his billfold and ID, as she protested, "I never said he knew where you were. I said he was *looking* for you. He said he'd just missed you in Pawhuska and had reason to believe you might be headed for Pawnee Town."

Longarm pursed his lips, considered that worked too many ways to pester the sweet old gal with, and settled for asking if she'd seen any ID to go with that other rider's story. He wasn't too surprised when she replied, sort of flustered, "I might have just jumped on his conclusions. He never said right out that he was the Law. He just had that bossy way about him, no offense. I didn't mean *you* acted bossy."

Longarm assured her he knew what she meant. He had no call to point out natural bullies could act mighty authoritative with even less of an excuse than a badge. He settled for asking her to describe the cuss better.

She thought, then decided. "Younger than he was trying to act. Late teens or early twenties. Brown hair with brown eyes. Dressed neat but sort of shabby, like a cowhand spruced up to spark with a nester's daughter. Seemed a nice enough young gent, in a sort of determined way, and oh, yes, he wore his Schofield .45 cross-draw, the way you're packing that Colt under your coat."

Longarm thanked her with a nod, but he was thinking too hard to say much as she wrapped all but the oats in paper, and twine for him. She must have been thinking too. For when she'd finished, she told him, "I think he said something about waiting for you in Pawnee Town. He said most everybody passing through this part of the Nation has to go through Pawnee Town, and that he, for one, was mighty weary of chasing you all over creation."

He thanked her again for her words of cheer and lugged his purchases out to the tethered ponies. He lashed the oats to the stock saddle and hung on to the rest for now. Then he led both ponies across the road and around that ball game to the back of the rambling, whitewashed complex he'd dismissed at first as simply an educational institution.

He didn't have to knock on any back door. One of those yellow dogs all the plains nations seemed to keep, came out from under the back steps to go into its mad-coyote act. It didn't even spook the ponies. Everyone knew Indians ate dogs that really bit before they ate anything else. A pretty young thing with long blond braids framing a mighty exotic face came out to call the dog off, anyway. As Longarm approached, leading his own dumb brutes, she called out, "He doesn't bite, sir. But, alas, I fear you've come at an awkward time."

Longarm stopped near the bottom of the steps to smile up at her uncertainly. Her big almond-shaped eyes were cornflower blue, and her suntanned skin was no darker than his own. But other than that she looked pure Pawnee.

This still left her pretty, albeit different from a heap of other blondes he'd met in his time. One reason the Pawnee had sided with the whites, aside from their abiding hatred of Cheyenne, had no doubt been the simple fact that like the Cherokee and most Iroquois the Pawnee had looked more natural to white folk, and vice versa. Some professors who worried about such matters said the so-called Indians had come to the New World from Old Siberia in waves of not too closely related hunting bands. They said that old Major Rogers, of Rogers's Rangers, had been shown a Greek statue over in London Town, only to exclaim, "My Gawd, they've gone and petrified a Mohawk!" And so, while this pretty little Pawnee didn't strike Longarm as an artifact carved from cold marble, he saw no way she might have been built better naturally. He felt sure she'd rather have him ask why he looked so awkward to her. So he did.

She said, "If you're looking for Mr. Wilson, our agent,

he just drove into Pawnee Town with his wife and daughter. I don't expect them back this side of Monday.''

Longarm smiled and said, ''Well, rank has its privileges, and who's to say a long weekend in the dog days of summer will bring the B.I.A. down in ruins, Miss . . . ah?''

''Singing Turtle, Herta Singing Turtle. I'm the school-teacher and agency nurse, as the need should arise.''

It would have been dumb to ask whether it had been her father or her mother who'd been German, so he never did. He just repeated what the old lady at the general store had told him about the agency having its own connection to the cross-country wires. She brightened and said, ''We certainly do, but again, alas, only Mr. Wilson knows how to send and receive Morse code.''

Longarm assured her she was wrong without going into too many old war stories, and so once they'd put his two ponies with the agency stock out back, she let him into the office she apparently got to share with the agent on the rare occasions he decided to put in a day's work. He wondered idly whether anyone at B.I.A. Headquarters knew Wilson had one ambitious breed gal wearing more than one hat out here in Pawnee country. But Billy Vail hadn't sent him to the Indian Nation to clean it up, and what the hell, there might be certain advantages to having the run of the premises while the lazy cat was away. As he sat himself down at the telegraph set he explained what he was about and added, ''Seeing you're a schoolmarm amongst other things, you'd know best who I'd want to wire first. Since this Friday afternoon is running down and most folk only work half a day tomorrow—''

''Are we talking about white kids attending B.I.A. schools?'' she cut in, and when he told her that was about the size of it, she explained, ''It's allowed. The agent's daughter, here, is in my fourth grade, and there are lots of other whites authorized to live on agency land. Too many, some say. But be that as it may, it's still unusual. So—''

''What if Lew and Adeline Dalton are squatting some-

148

where, claiming long-lost Indian kin?'' he cut in.

To which she replied with a sigh, "We'd best just ask the recording secretary of each school board in the Nation, then. If any pupils named Dalton are enrolled in any school betwixt here and Fort Smith under their right names—''

He hushed her with, "Gotcha. And that's what I meant about you knowing more than me about Indian schools. I don't have to get in touch with each and every school as long as I can wire the central board at each agency, right?''

She produced a B.I.A. directory, giving the names and addresses he'd need to prove or disprove that particular notion. But when he asked if she knew who ran schools around Kingfisher, she confessed she wouldn't bet her own money there was any infernal school there. So, figuring that chore studied to be the most tedious, he fed some battery juice to the agency key and cut into the Western Union traffic. He only caught a few minutes of the usual guff before an old hand down the line sent: "ITS NO USE BOYS STOP I RECOGNIZE THE FIST STOP IT'S THAT LONGARM ON OUR LINE STOP BEST LET HIM HAVE HIS WAY SO WESTERN UNION CAN HAVE ITS WIRE BACK STOP''

Longarm didn't recall the call letters of the wiseass, but they worked on the other telegraphers who'd been giving him a hard time. So he began by asking Western Union's advice as well as consent. They agreed it would save time and trouble for all concerned if he'd let them track down the infernal Dalton kids for him. There could only be so many school boards in the Indian Nation and the newer Oklahoma Territory combined. He sent that he'd stand by. He meant it. But as he leaned back in the bentwood chair and asked Herta's permission to light up, that dog under the back steps commenced to bark again. So she said she'd go see who or what it might be this time.

He started to go after her. But he'd just told Western Union he was standing by, and what the hell, she could always scream if it was anything bad, right?

149

He got back on the wire and told Western Union they could send anything about the damned little Daltons at, say, suppertime. Then he got up and ambled back along the corridor to catch Herta talking with a more Indian-looking Indian in the kitchen. The hatchet-faced cuss was seated at her table, and when she spied Longarm in the doorway, she allowed he could have coffee and cake as soon as it was ready.

Herta introduced the blue-clad Indian in the big black hat as her cousin, Calvin Fishing Wolf. The Pawnee shook firm and friendly, saying, "Heard you was on the reserve. You're the one I rid out to talk to. I ride for the Pawnee Police."

Longarm said he'd noticed the army-blue shirt and resisted the impulse to ask whether Fishing Wolf's hair was roached Pawnee-style under that big old hat. Instead he just said, "Now that you've found me, what do you want to talk about?"

Fishing Wolf said soberly, "How come you seem so popular? The old postmistress across the way told me you might be here. The cuss who said he was looking for you never showed up down the line in Pawnee Town. That's not saying he's not watching the road betwixt here and there from some handy clump of cottonwood. If so, he's good. I was watching as I rid up, and I don't like to brag, but—"

"When did Pawnee learn not to brag?" Longarm cut in with a smile. It was a friendly smile. So Fishing Wolf smiled back and said, "All right, if the rascal's laying for you out there, he's *really* good. Let's talk about that Cheyenne breed you gunned over on the other side of Pawhuska. We always get the news sort of distorticated from the Osage."

Longarm laughed and said that was for certain. Then Herta shoved sponge cake and coffee in front of both of them. So Longarm got to nibble and sip as he filled the Indian officer in on that Cheyenne breed planted just a mite shallow by Miss Martha Tipisota, leaving out Miss Wynona

150

Widington and other dirty parts entirely. When he added, "I never met old Ben. Don't even recall his last name, if anyone ever mentioned it to me to begin with."

Fishing Wolf seemed sincerely puzzled as he replied, "Now that's really odd, unless we're suffering a plague of pesky Cheyenne where they've got no business being. I could be wrong, but the story both you and the Osage seem to agree on agrees with our official report on one Benedict Mason, a recent graduate of Colorado State, and we ain't talking about the college. We chased him out of Pawnee Town once he bragged on being part Cheyenne, like that was something to brag on!"

Longarm chuckled and said, "He might not have been up on the old blood feud betwixt you boys and Those Who Cut Off Fingers."

Fishing Wolf grimaced and declared, "He called his red kin Tsitsita. That's how we knew he meant it."

Longarm nodded agreeably, no Tsitsita being present, and inhaled more cake and coffee before he observed, "It sounds as if the breed, Martha Tipisota, was so vexed with what might have annoyed folk in Pawnee Town, first. But what connection did you figure I might have with a saddle bum I never saw, alive or otherwise?"

The Pawnee said, "After we told him to leave Pawnee Town for his health, the ones called Babe and Larch rode in, asking for him. There was another one, answering to the name Beaumont, who said he was a friend the Cheyenne breed had agreed to meet in Pawnee Town. When he was told Mason had ridden on, he asked if *you* had passed through. He asked for you by name, Deputy Marshal Custis Long."

Longarm whistled and softly replied, "Old Boulder Bill sure acted like he'd come a long ways looking for me, and I could have been wrong the time I thought I was rescuing a lady in distress, but hold on, when did you boys chase

Mason off this particular reserve and on what charge, by the way?''

The Pawnee policeman looked uncomfortable and confided, "My boss thought it was for his own good. We told him so. He didn't kick up much of a fuss once we'd pointed out how many scalp locks, took by both sides, were still showed off on ceremonious occasions.''

Fishing Wolf pursed his lips and counted in his head a spell before he decided. "Must have been six or eight weeks ago that pesky Cheyenne breed was disturbing the peace in Pawnee Town. Is the exact date important?''

Longarm shook his head and replied, "You couldn't be off by more than a month, and it just won't work if you are. Martha Tipisota said the breed had been pestering her a spell before he, ah, took sick and passed away. It's good to hear she was telling me true about him, and the three I saved her from arrived well ahead of me, so . . .''

"They might have known you were coming,'' Herta said, trying to explain as both men stared blankly at her. "That other one knew you'd pass through Ralston long before you got here, didn't he?''

Fishing Wolf nodded and said, "She's got a point. Hear me, there are only so many trails a man can take, and if enough enemies are expecting him—''

"That's a swampsome heap of enemies.'' Longarm objected, adding, "It gets even murkier as soon as you consider that neither me nor anyone from my home office knew, or could have known, I'd be headed this way to begin with! The breed called Mason must have been dead before I left Denver!''

Fishing Wolf pointed out, "His pals didn't know that, if they were searching for him just ahead of you. They might have thought you were after *him*, trailing *them*, or . . . You know, you're right! Whatever you think you're doing here in the Nation, you've surely turned over a heap of wet rocks, and I'm having a time keeping track of all the wiggle worms!''

Longarm sighed and said, "If you're keeping track of *any,* you're doing way better than me. Far be it from me to criticize the way this odd part of the country is run, but all in all I find my job a heap easier when I get to mess with pale-faced outlaws or hostile redskins, no offense."

Fishing Wolf said, "None taken. No *Indian* ever came up with anything as confused or confusing as the B.I.A., or the way Washington keeps cutting this patchwork quilt apart and sewing it back together different. It's not hard to wind up with red and white neighbors at peace or at feud when every time a new party gets in back East, they change the rules. Look how they just threw everything west of the Stillwater stage stop open to white settlers, for Andrew Jackson's sake!"

Longarm protested, "Don't look at me. Things were even worse under Grant. I helped clean the old Indian Ring Scandal up. The new settlement of Kingfisher would be in the paler parts of Oklahoma Territory now, right?"

Calvin Fishing Wolf nodded, but when Longarm asked if they might have anything on the Daltons or any other members of their far-flung clan, the Indian policeman just looked pained and said, "Let's not worry about Frank and Jesse this far west, Longarm. We have enough on our plates with our homegrown outlaws, red *and* white."

Longarm nodded, said Judge Parker over to Fort Smith had said much the same thing. But then he insisted, "Assuming a horse dealer called Dingus Howard is long gone, if he ever was important, I was still sent down this way to catch up with and question Adeline Dalton née Younger, and if my being here upsets you boys, you'll be rid of me sooner if you help me locate the durned Daltons. So about the last tip I got as to their present whereabouts . . ."

"I don't know," insisted Fishing Wolf, rising to his feet as he added, "I can ask, as soon as I get back to Pawnee Town. But we have no jurisdiction as far west as Kingfisher, and you know how silly some small-town lawmen can get about Indians even asking for a *drink.*"

Longarm rose, too, to shake on it. He said, "If you'd care to wait till I get some answers to some questions I was just asking by wire, I'd be proud to ride down to Pawnee Town with you."

Calvin Fishing Wolf smiled impishly and confided, "My chief will have a fit if you do. He hates noise. I know I can't stop you, and I could use the company on the trail. But I don't want to get there after dark, and I'm barely going to make it if I leave right now."

So Longarm helped Herta clear the table instead, even though she said that was woman's work and that her Pawnee kinsmen would poke fun at any man they saw behaving so sissy.

He chuckled and suggested, "Let's not tell 'em, then. What they don't know won't hurt any of us. If you'd like to wash, I'm willing to dry."

She laughed incredulously, called him a big goof, and said there'd be plenty of dishes to wash and dry if he felt up to hanging around until suppertime.

He said he had to, explaining, "I might even be stuck longer, if Western Union lets us down. As I told you before, I'm trying to save me and the ponies a heap of dumb riding back and forth. I'd just be wasting battery juice as well if I lit out before locating the infernal Daltons scientifically. So even though I may seem to be shirking my duty here—"

She cut in with "Heavens! Nobody said anything about you riding on before suppertime, or even afterwards. I told you we had the whole place to ourselves for a whole weekend, and it's not as if I enjoy my own company that much. So if they don't locate those white folk for you before sundown and you'd like to spend the night . . ."

Longarm said he surely would, and since they were standing side by side, he figured he might as well reel her in to prove it.

She kissed back, mighty French for a Pawnee-German gal, and she even let him pat her down a mite for concealed weapons, but as they came up for air she was blushing like a rose and demanding, "What's got into you, Custis? I only meant we've got us a mess of spare rooms here. I hope you didn't think I meant what I just said the way some mighty wild and wicked gals indeed might have meant it."

He sighed and said, "*I* was sort of hoping you might. I'd have kissed you more sedate if I'd thought otherwise. Are you aware of the parts of me your rubbing them parts of you against, ma'am?"

She rubbed harder, kissing him as if to shut him up as she proved she knew just what she was doing with her thrustworthy pubic bone. He hadn't thought he was the one talking dumb. So he eased them into an even more tempting position, with her tailbone against the edge of the drainboard, before he gently proceeded to hitch her summerweight calico up a handful at a time. He only got her skirts halfway hoisted before she protested, her lips against his, "For land's sake, standing up, before suppertime?"

To which he could only reply, "We just had cake and coffee, and I'd rather sup late than indulge in indoor sports on an overstuffed gut. But if you'd rather go on from here in a less ridiculous stance . . ."

She replied with a moan and one thigh hooked over the grips of his .44-40 as she rose tiptoe on the other foot, to line things up a mite better.

She wasn't wearing anything under her dress. That still left a dire amount of his infernal tweed betwixt them, and in truth, she hadn't managed to move high enough. So he quickly shucked his coat, and as it fell to the kitchen floor behind him he got an elbow under each of her knees to perch her on the kitchen drainboard in a mighty bawdy position, had anyone been peeking in at them. But since nobody was, Herta was a good sport about unbuttoning his pants and getting that barrier to romance out of the way as well. But as she took what he had to offer in hand, to guide it where they both seemed to want it, she gasped and demanded, "My God, are you expecting me to take all of

155

this?'' And then she gasped even louder and moaned, ''Oh, Jesus, I see you are, and it feels so good! But don't you think it might feel better if we did it less awkwardly in bed?''

Longarm agreed that sounded reasonable. So that was where they wound up, before sundown, albeit they tore off an interesting experiment on the kitchen table as he was sort of packing her off to the bedroom on his saddle horn, as she insisted on calling it.

Chapter 17

Another nice thing about making love before most folk all about were having supper was that he got to sit in the office bare-assed, with a naked blonde in his lap, sharing a smoke with the same as he took down telegraph messages from all over creation. The Cherokee school board in Vinita hadn't even gotten his earlier wire, since nobody seemed to be there. But whether the Daltons had moved to the Cherokee Strip or not, they weren't sending their brood to any Osage, Pawnee, Ponka, or Kansas schools. Herta said there was a lot of bootlegging down in the Muskogee, or Creek, country. Longarm explained he'd already wired the reserves to the south but added, "Aside from the fact they ain't answered yet, I doubt Lew Dalton would wander that deep into Indian country. He likes to take advantage of Indians. I don't think he gets along too well with 'em."

She wriggled her bare butt into a more comfortable, or certainly more interesting, position as she pointed out, "Didn't you say he'd been run out of Missouri first and then Kansas by other palefaces, dear?"

He nodded but said, "His troubles with his neighbors seem to stem more from unpaid bills than a surly nature. It's tough to lose money running saloons, but he manages, competing with other whites. He'd no doubt have to quit

157

entire and go find some honest job if it wasn't for the B.I.A. liquor regulations being so dumb that even a dunce can make out sneaking mighty expensive firewater to you poor innocents.''

She reached down between her bare thighs to see what could be done about the innocent way his semi-erection seemed to be aimed as she confided, ''The nice thing about being half German is that I only have to act innocent when I'm signing for my B.I.A. handouts.''

The telegraph set on the nearby table was clicking again. So he told her to take her hand the hell out of there as he reached for a pencil stub and began to transcribe the dots and dashes into block letters on the bitty blue pad. She seemed to think it was funny to jerk his poor dong in time with the telegraph key, and it was clicking fast as hell. So even as he was taking down the last of the message from Kingfisher she was leaning forward, away from him, with her bare feet braced on the floor, wide apart, pleading, ''Move your ass, won't you?'' as she moved her own, with him barely in her again.

That was no way to treat a lady. So he rose to the occasion and they finished on their feet with her bent over to grasp her own trim ankles as he braced her naked rump with one hand, holding the wire from Kingfisher with the other as he read it. She seemed to take it as a personal insult when he growled, ''Goddammit, folk have no right to screw so careless.''

When she arched her spine to take him deeper, asking if that felt careful enough, he laughed and said, ''I ain't talking about us. I mean Lew and Adeline Dalton. They *did* have their kids in school at Kingfisher. All but the oldest ones, leastways. Only just last week they've pulled the poor little tykes out again. Seems Lew Dalton's moving on some more. He never said where. You'd think such shiftless folk would take at least some precautions if they just don't care about raising kids right. What's to become of all those little

158

Daltons if they just grow up like Topsy, with no schooling at all?"

She suggested, "The boys can all grow up to be crooks like their dad, and the gals can all grow up to be bodacious screwers, like their mama must be, and speaking of bodacious screwing, could we go back to bed some more, now that you're done fooling with that telegraph?"

He said he wasn't finished yet. But he finished with her, for the time being, before he sat back down to get off a light letter to his home office. Herta didn't distract him this time. She said all that slap and tickle had made her hungry and that he'd find her in the kitchen if he wanted to try out that table again, either way.

The light was getting tricky in the little office now. He thought about lighting the oil lamp hanging above the agent's rolltop desk. He decided not to when he looked for a window shade as well and saw there wasn't any. He knew how dumb he'd appear to anyone passing by outside. So, faced with the choice of getting all the way dressed again or sending and receiving Morse in the dark, he settled for the dark. When he rejoined Herta in the kitchen, he saw great minds ran in the same channels. She'd poked up the fire and stuck more stove wood in the cast-iron range, but save for the faint glow and occasional flare she made rustling up their late supper, the kitchen stayed dark enough to convince anyone just passing that nobody at all was home that evening. He figured she wanted to give the impression as soon as he noticed that she was cooking with nothing but her apron on. The apron she'd slipped on to protect her more delicate parts from stove splatters only served to make her bare parts seem bore bawdy. But Longarm didn't mind. He suspected he'd need all the inspiration he could get, having started so early in the evening with such a lusty young lady. So he studied her Indian hips and Germanic behind with malice aforethought as he sat at the table, smoking in his own birthday suit.

As if she'd read his mind, she giggled and said she'd

159

never live it down if someone were to walk in on her, fixing supper so informally.

He said soothingly, "That dog out back ought to bar you fair warning, and you did lock yonder door, didn' you?"

She said she thought she might have. He thought he' best make sure. So he rose to his bare feet and ambled ove to the back door. He found the bolt in place. As he absentl glanced out at the dark backyard he thought he sensed move ment until, squinting closer, he got all the shadow betwix the back steps and the stable across the yard to hold stil Neither the dog under the house nor the stock out back wer fussing at anyone or anything, and critters were better detecting trespassers in tricky light. So he went back to th table and sat down some more.

He still felt compelled to ask how often other gents cam calling of an evening in these parts. Herta sighed and said "You'd still have your pants on if I was expecting company The agent and his womenfolk have a few white friends i and about Ralston. My Pawnee cousins seem to feel lik my German cousins when it comes to socializing with hal breeds."

He was tempted to tell her she was likely wrong abou that. It would have been a lie. So he never. He'd met to many folk of the red, white, and in-between persuasions t go along with the superstition that miscengenation bre monsters with the worse traits of both races. But he kne a heap of folk did—red, white, and the unfortunate victim of the slander themselves.

He had a tougher time keeping his thoughts to himsel once the pretty half Pawnee put his supper to table befor him. For there were gals who were pretty all over, ther were gals who screwed swell, and there were gals wh cooked this good. But finding three such prizes wrapped i one sweet hide was mighty rare, and any of the local hand who figured on finding better in such empty country wer suffering optimism past all common sense.

160

She'd made him potato pancakes and some meat dish as tasted like pickled pigs' feet but looked like roast beef. She said it had been her German mama who'd taught her to put whipped cream in coffee as well. Longarm generally took his coffee black. But it could have been worse. Had her mama been the Indian parent, likely they'd have been drinking coffee with white flour stirred into it and that was *really* an acquired taste.

The coffee, strong as well as sweet, combined with bare nipples dimly lit across the table to inspire him to serve her a swell, fresh erection for dessert, once he'd carried her, giggling, back to the bedroom. But being a woman, once she'd had her wicked way with him and he just wanted to lay there blowing smoke rings for a spell, she had to pester him some more about them being caught in such embarrassing proximity. He sighed and said, "Just let me get my fool breath back, and I'll just be dressed and on my way, ma'am."

She grabbed his flaccid manhood, as if that were the best way to hang on to him, and she pleaded, "Oh, no, don't leave me! The night is young, and you're expecting more telegraph messages in the morning, remember?"

He said he sure did but added, "I could always come by again with my duds on after a campout on the range, you know. You should have told me you were married, or at least expecting company, before you ever let me kiss you, ma'am."

She sobbed. "You know I've had nobody but you for an awfully long, lonely time, darling. I'll just die if you don't do me dirty tonight and at least through tomorrow night. I don't *expect* anyone back from Pawnee Town before Monday. When you're in me, I don't *care* whether they come back or not. But between times, thinking calm about how long it took me to get this job, even with a degree from Carlyle . . ."

He cut in with "Bless your bottom. Did you really graduate from that college as takes Indians, free, back East?"

She answered simply, "I had to. Carlyle's the only institution of higher learning open to us naked savages."

He chuckled fondly, told her he liked her to act savage when she was naked, and then he said, "Look, if you're really feeling all that proddy about someone walking in on us here, why don't we bed down somewhere more private?"

When she objected that there was no place half as safe as where they were, in a hamlet the size of Ralston, he said, "Sure there is. I got a bedroll tied to my McClellan, and there's much to be said for a firm surface under your sweet, sweet rump as I runs it in and out of your sweet little ring-dang-do."

She jerked his limp love tool teasingly as she giggled and answered, "Promises, promises, and where could we act so bawdy under the stars without having to worry about someone tripping over us in the act, across the Arkansas on the Osage range?"

He shook his head and said, "Osage laugh just as hard when they catch folk screwing. I was thinking of under the house."

She laughed and told him he was crazy before she considered his suggestion enough to matter. Then she said, "You know, that makes a lot more sense as soon as you think about it. Nobody ever looks under the back steps but Rex, and I don't care what *he* thinks about my private life."

So they sat up and got dressed, enough to go out back in the dark, at least. She used the outhouse while Longarm fetched the bedroll from the stable and crawled under the agency with it. The dog, Rex, seemed more confused than growly as Longarm struck a match to make sure there were no dog turds, black widows, or skunk nests too close to where he unrolled the bedding on the bare soil under the crawl space. Once he had, he tried sitting upright and discovered that while that wouldn't work, there was plenty of room for movement, even with her on top, as long as she didn't stick her head too high and mighty as she bounced.

Once she'd crawled under there with him, giggling like

162

a schoolkid swiping apples after dark, he excused himself to use the backyard facilities as well. He'd just done so and shaken the dew from the lily when he heard hoofbeats in the middle distance. Sounded more like two riders than a carriage team. Likely cowhands going somewheres. Ralston wasn't what you could really call anywheres in particular.

He dropped to his hands and knees to crawl back under the agency. Once he had he found Herta had tied the poor dog under the back steps and gotten out of her duds and into his bedroll. As he put his gun in his overturned hat and shucked the rest of his outfit to join her, the dog whimpered at them. He asked how come she'd tied it so cruel, and she modestly replied, "I don't want Rex sticking his cold nose in here with us."

Longarm laughed and said, "I don't think I'd like that, neither."

She began to hump him, slow and sensuous, as she softly smiled and decided, "I'd want to do this with at least two of you if you weren't so sweet about making it last."

He didn't tell her how easy it was to keep from coming right now. He sure wanted to, and that strong coffee helped, but starting before sundown might have been a tactical error if she really expected him to keep at it all night.

Fortunately she was made of clay as mortal, and not only climaxed ahead of him but began to beg for mercy as he kept trying to catch up. He was at that stage where he didn't know whether he was about to come or go soft and one part of him kept telling him to quit, while another swore it would never forgive him if he did.

The victim of all this confusion pleaded, "Don't hold back, dear. You've satisfied me completely. I just want you to come so we can get some well deserved rest, see?"

He saw. So he faked it. Women weren't the only ones who could be polite and just lay there, marinating it in her love juices as he tried to get his second wind. She protested,

163

"I'm getting a kink in one hip. Can I put my legs down at least?"

Before he could answer, the dog let out a howl that would have done credit to a timber wolf. So she hugged him even harder with her thighs, gasping, "Oh, God, someone's coming!"

Longarm had already snatched up his .44-40. He whispered, "Unwrap your sweet self from my bare ass and let me get *at* the son of a bitch, then!"

She whispered, "On, no, don't leave me! I'm so scared, and good grief, I'm either fixing to piddle or come!"

He growled, "Don't do neither just now, girl! I make it two of 'em out back. They've dismounted by the stable. Listen, hear them spurs headed our way?"

She wasn't even listening to him. She was writhing under him in passion, biting her own lower lip to keep from letting the whole world know it as she told him with her internal contractions just how hard she was coming this time. And to Longarm's mild surprise he seemed to be coming himself. It sure felt wild, and he almost fired his double-action Colt before he had enough sense to slip his twitch finger off the trigger just in time.

As he lay still atop her, save for the pulsations inside her and the way both their hearts still pounded, the one with the spurs banged the back door and shouted, "We know you're in there, Longarm!"

The girl he was really in stiffened and might have cried out, had he not crushed her lips with his free palm and whispered, "He's talking about the rooms above us, not your you-know. Lie still and let's just listen!"

So they did. The one at the back door was joined by someone who clumped more than he jingled. The newcomer's voice was higher pitched as he called out, "That Tennessee Walker they told us about is sure enough in yonder stable. Sure looks like the one Dingus was riding that time."

The one wearing spurs replied, "We wouldn't be here if a cuss answering to Longarm's looks and a pony answering to the one Dingus rode hadn't been seen here, and only here at this river crossing, you fool kid!''

The one clumping around protested, ''Watch who you calls a fool, big brother. Had not I overheard them Pawnee lawmen, you'd still be waiting for the big galoot in Pawnee Town, where he ain't.''

This time Herta didn't try to stop him as Longarm warily rolled off her to haul on his pants. But as he reached for his shirt in the dark they heard the back door open, right above them, and when she hissed, ''I locked that door behind us, Custis!'' he muttered, ''Help me with my boots, will you? Locked doors are unimportant details to riders of the owl-hoot trail, and neither one of those boys sound at all like Pawnee Police to me!''

She agreed they couldn't be anyone she knew as one clumped around inside and the other apparently stood guard in the kitchen, just inside the back door. By the time the one who'd let himself in came back, growling, ''Nobody at all in the place. Want some sponge cake?'' Herta got to feel indignant about that on her lonesome. For Longarm had already rolled away in the dark in his boots, pants, shirt, and six-gun rig, aiming to exit the crawl space on the darker side of the agency.

Thus it came to pass that as the two teenage riders hunting him headed back for their own tethered ponies, they couldn't even find them. The one wearing the spurs said, ''What the hell . . . ?'' before he spied the rump of his paint where Longarm had retethered it and added, ''Oh, yonder they be. I could have sworn we left 'em out here where it's more open.''

Then, as they stepped into the shadows after their ponies, Longarm assured them pleasantly, from behind, ''You did. Now you're both going to keep staring straight ahead as you unbuckle them gun rigs and let 'em fall. If you try anything dumber, you're both dead. Do we understand each other, boys?''

165

The shorter and slighter of the two whispered, "What are we going to do, Frank?"

His older and way smarter brother sighed and said, "Like the man says, of course. They told us he was good, but this is ridiculous!"

So a few moments later Longarm had the two teenagers disarmed and back out in the moonlight where he could get a better look at them. Neither one impressed him much. The younger one looked somewhere between sixteen and eighteen. The older reminded Longarm how young and innocent he'd been that time he ran off to a war nobody had even invited him to. Longarm nodded grimly but not unkindly as he said, "I started young too. I know you boys have been looking for me. Are you anybody I'm supposed to be looking for? No offense, but neither of you answers the description of Billy the Kid, and nobody else as wet behind the ears is on my current list."

The younger one put on a brave face and declared, "I'd be Grat Dalton, and this here's my brother, Frank. Don't go getting wise with us just because you got the drop on us, sneaky. You ain't messing with white trash when you mess with the Dalton boys. Aside from our many other brothers, we got kin you don't want to mess with, neither, see?"

Before Longarm could answer, Frank Dalton snapped, "Shut your fool face, Grat! Don't tell the lawman you're a total asshole. Let him figure it out for himself, hear?"

Longarm glanced at the gun rigs, on the ground some distance away, as he decided, "We may as well all sit down and take a load off our brains, boys. You know where the back door is. You just now slipped the spring lock in a manner that bodes ill for the more honest folk you meet up with in the future. I'll tell you whether I'm arresting you after I hear your sad stories."

They were in no position to argue. So they didn't. In the meantime Herta had been smart enough to slip into her summer-weight dress and beat the three of them into her kitchen. As he herded the Dalton boys inside she started to light the lamp. Longarm told her not to, explaining, "Not until I sort out just how many rascals are gunning for me and why. But I reckon these boys would enjoy some of that swell German coffee you make, seeing they rid up from Pawnee Town so intent this evening."

As Herta heated up the coffee Longarm asked the Dalton brothers why they'd been acting so intent, adding, "You may as well know I can prove you were asking for me earlier, right here in Ralston, whichever one of you it was. I see you both have brown eyes and brown hair."

Frank Dalton said, "It was me. Grat, here, only tagged along this evening. You ain't got nothing on him or anyone else in my family, you nosy cuss."

Longarm nodded and replied, "Never said I did. What might I have on you, Frank? Have you been gunning for me with good reason or just for the hell of it?"

Young Grat sneered. "Everyone knows you're out to collect the bounty on Cousin Dingus, you son of a— Sorry, ma'am, I forgot ladies was present."

Frank Dalton swore harder, albeit under his breath, and kicked his baby brother under the table as he hissed, "He ain't that close a cousin if he's kin at all, and it's talk like that draws the law like flies to our poor mama's sweet, innocent head, you fool kid!"

Turning back to Longarm, he continued. "If I was to tell you the infernal truth, it wouldn't inspire you to leave our mama alone, would it?"

His remark had been more a statement of opinion than a question, but Longarm still replied, "You might try me. You heard right when you heard I was looking for your mother, Adeline Dalton née Younger, in connection with the present whereabouts of Buck and Dingus or Frank and Jesse James. I've got a black pony out back who says that either one who passed through here a spell back has, well, passed through."

Grat Dalton said, "Our folk don't know which way anyone went. It ain't right to pester Mama about it. She cries when the law comes to pester her, and she don't even *like* Cousin Dingus."

Frank Dalton nodded soberly and said, "That's the pure and simple truth. Mama's a Younger, not a James, and you got all the Youngers who ever robbed anyone in jail. It's no secret Mama sends cakes she may have baked and socks she may had knit to Cousins Cole and Bob in the Minnesota State Pen. What if she does? They're allowed to accept such modest comforts, and she's their dead dad's only sister."

Herta served the coffee as Longarm said soothingly, "Nobody said your mother can't be nice to her imprisoned nephews, Frank. It's aiding and abetting bank robbers still at large that the law frowns upon."

Frank nodded and said, "That's what I told old Dingus to his face, over to Pawhuska over a month ago. He rid in pretending he was a horse trader, and what did them fool Osage know? Oops, sorry, ma'am."

Herta said Pawnee didn't think much of Osage, either. Longarm shot her a warning look and insisted, "Never mind all that, Frank. You admit you met up with Jesse James in the flesh that recent?"

Frank Dalton shrugged and said, "I had to. He was asking the way to our dad's, ah, wayside inn near Kingfisher. I reckon he figured nobody would look for him that far west. I told him he was likely right. Then I told him I'd gun him down like a dog if he went one country mile closer to my mama and little sisters."

As Longarm stared dubiously at the grim-faced youth, young Grat grinned and said, "He would have too. Ask anyone in the Nation if they've ever seen any Dalton back down."

Frank Dalton said more modestly, "I don't think Dingus was afraid to shoot it out with me. Like I was hoping, he was too smart to. He knew our mama would never take him in after he'd shot one of her children. So once he saw there was no way to get to her without going over my dead body,

he just figured the game wasn't worth the candle and headed
. . . don't ask if you don't want us to lie to you.''

Longarm frowned thoughtfully and decided, ''Your story
jibes with some others I've heard. I can see why an outlaw
way off his usual stomping grounds would suddenly need
traveling money. He'd hesitate to pull outright robberies,
having no place to seek certain shelter. So that accounts for
him selling the same horse sort of tedious and . . . hold on,
somebody has to be lying like a rug around here!''

Herta, who'd naturally been listening, opined that everything young Frank had said made sense to her as she doled
out more sponge cake and the forks as went with it.

Longarm explained, ''I'm not saying these boys are lying.
Others bear out their story of a mysterious horse trader who's
no longer with us. It's how long he *ain't* been with us that
I find mysterious.''

All three of them stared blankly at him in the dim light.
Longarm said, ''Frank, if you chased an unwanted house-
guest east from the Osage Strip, long before I even got
there, who's been working so hard to stop me from catching
up with any of you Daltons way west of any place Jesse
James could be right now?''

The two brothers exchanged cautious glances. Frank
washed down some of Herta's sponge cake and said, ''Heck,
we haven't been trying all that hard. I've been working on
the Rogers' Spread, over in the Cherokee Strip. When the
folk writ me, they were being pestered by bill collectors in
Kingfisher and might just move over to Vinita to join me,
I naturally headed for home to help 'em with the mule teams
and such, most of our brothers and sisters being still a mite
tiny to be much help.''

Longarm said, ''An Osage told me you'd been working
near Vinita. I may owe him an apology too. All you just
told me took place after you warned Jesse he might not be
welcome in Kingfisher?''

Frank Dalton nodded and said, ''I said it was a month
or more ago I had that out with Dingus. I only heard about

169

you as I was passing through the Osage Strip a day or so
back. I didn't want you pestering Mama. I rid after you to
head you off. Meanwhile the folks had headed east. So
when I met 'em this afternoon in Pawnee Town and they
said you hadn't pestered 'em, I knew you couldn't have got
that far yet. Me and this tagalong kid brother backtracked
to the crossing here, heard from the old lady at the store
you might be over here at the agency, and the rest you
know.''

Herta Singing Turtle said it seemed clear as crystal to
her. Longarm asked if he could have more coffee, without
the whipped cream, and confided, ''It's clear as mud to me.
If I take it that neither of these boys have been really serious
about stopping me, and allow the nonsense with Nitro Nick
and the Woodson boys was no more than that—pure nonsense—it still leaves those more serious attacks on me.''

Since the Dalton boys seemed sincerely ignorant of at
least half his recent misadventures, Longarm quickly
brought them up-to-date, and they agreed he had every right
to feel perplexed.

Frank Dalton said, ''I can't tell you where Buck and
Dingus are, save for it not being anywheres near the Nation,
and you have my word on that.''

Longarm said, ''Word taken. But that gets us back to
more than one would-be assassin I've firmly established as
a gun for hire. I hope you boys won't take this wrong, but
I can't see anyone in the Dalton clan sending away for such
help and then sending two teenagers to bar my way to
Pawnee Town. The James boys are more prone to do their
own killing, but again, they'd have to be somewhere in the
infernal vicinity if they were afraid of my discovering where.
Wipe that cake off your chin, Grat, and be advised that I'm
not just taking the word of any one or two in these parts.
Someone's been trying to stop me from finding something
else out. Something as has nothing to do with anyone named
Dalton, Younger or James.''

170

Herta brightened and said, "It must have been that attempted safecracking in Pawhuska!"

Longarm shook his head and said, "If Nitro Nick had been at all worried about me coming, he'd have never been trying to crack that safe with me in town. He couldn't have known I was in town, or if he did, he couldn't have been all that worried about me. The trouble I got into with his even dumber confederates in Gray Horse was just as dumb as it sounds. So scratch the Woodsons as well as the Daltons, Youngers, and James Brothers and . . . we're sort of scraping the bottom of the barrel, ain't we?"

Frank Dalton shoved his plate away and said, "That surely was swell, ma'am," before he turned back to Longarm to add, "I'd sure like to solve the mystery for you. I've considered taking up the law as a career my ownself, but when I applied over to Fort Smith, they said to come back when I was a mite older. Are we straight, now, seeing you know better than to pester our mama needless?"

Longarm said, "I may need to pester her, I may not. It depends on some answers to some questions I asked earlier this evening, in Morse code. Your folk will surely be crossing the Arkansas here at Ralston on their way east, won't they, Frank?"

The youth stared stubbornly at Longarm and replied, "They might. They might just cross downstream at, say, Creek Town. I ain't sure I like your attitude, Longarm. I told you to leave my mama alone, and I meant what I said."

Longarm sighed and said, "I know. It's a bad habit you'd best break soon, old son. We just agreed on the sensible reasons Jesse James might have had for sparing your mama's feelings. I'm just too sweet-natured for my own good. That's why I'm not pistol-whipping you silly for trying to crawfish me in front of a woman with your own guns way out in the moonlight."

Frank Dalton growled grudgingly. "You got the upper hand right now. I just said we was straight until such time as you try to pester my innocent mama. When and if you do, and I'm there, you might not get the drop on me again as easy.''

Longarm nodded soberly and said, ''I sure admire your brass, kid. Can't say all that much for your brains. If you'd like to run home to your mama now, I won't gun you as your ride out, as long as you just keep riding.''

The elder of the still mighty young Dalton brothers hesitated, then got to his feet, saying ''Our pleasure, ma'am. Come on, Grat.'' And then Longarm and Herta were alone again.

The blond Pawnee heaved a deep sigh of relief and said, ''I just hate to hear men growl, Custis. Do you reckon you're going to have to kill that nice-looking one?''

Longarm flatly stated, ''If I pester his mother, I'll likely have to. Fortunately, the way things are starting to add up, I may not have to. I don't think she knows beans about Frank and Jesse James, and as her boy just said, it seems mean to pester a lady for no good reason.''

Herta said, ''Goody. Let's go back under the house and I'll give you a swell reason to pester *me*.''

Chapter 18

Whether the mills of justice ground fine or not, they ground exceedingly slow in the opinion of Marshal Billy Vail. For here it was, long after his boys had brought Wee Willy Wiggins in from the high country for trial, and the fool federal courts were still fooling with the little shit.

Vail wouldn't have minded half as much if they hadn't called upon him and his deputies to attend all the pre-trial powwows it took just to try one worthless polecat. Vail had known from the time he'd sent that detail out to pick the prisoner up that the case was open-and-shut, with all the evidence pointing to a short dance at the end of a long rope. Yet here Vail stood again in the marble halls of the Denver Federal Building, making sure there were no slipups, as Smiley and Dutch brought Wiggins yet again from his detention cell while Guilfoyle and Flynn were posted with their 10-gauges at each stairwell and Deputies Cohan and Vandermeer kept their eyes on things inside the courtroom.

Vail wasn't sure why. It was true that the *Post* and the *Rocky Mountain News* were following the case with lip-smacking interest, and it was true that folk had come down to Denver from all over the mining country to make certain Wee Willy caught what was coming to him. But there'd been no escape attempts or serious demonstrations during the protracted pre-trial bullshit, and as they got set this morning to start the no-shit jury trial at last, Vail sensed a heap of others were as tired of the case as he was. For there wasn't much of a crowd inside, and not too many more seemed to be arriving as the hour approached.

Knowing it couldn't be as late in the day as it felt, Vail hauled out his pocket watch, consulted it, and permitted himself a frosty smile as he saw he'd been a mite pessimistic about the time, after all. He pocketed his watch and grumped down to the nearest stairwell. He told the deputy posted there, "The trial's about to start. I want you boys and your scatterguns to either side of the doorway now. So pass it on to Flynn and make sure nobody gets inside without a pass from the court clerk. Any questions?"

Guilfoyle answered, "It's likely no business of mine, boss, but is it fair to hold a murder trial with the press and public barred from the courtroom?"

Vail said, "Wee Willy ain't on trial for murder alone. Before he murdered Emma Ferguson he raped her, more than once and in more ways than one. Before he murdered her husband, Hamish, he welshed on his word about money, in mining country. So the judge is *letting* the little shit have an open trial, as long as nobody who might want to take the law into his own hands is allowed within pistol range of our prisoner. The newspaper reporters, and anyone else who wants to watch, are free to do so, provided they apply a day early in writing to the court clerk. We don't want just anybody wandering in during the course of the trial with Lord knows what under his coat, see?"

Guilfoyle shrugged, then tensed a mite to softly say, "Something coming up them stairs at us, boss."

Vail said to hold his fire for now. They were glad Guilfoyle had, when a familiar pancaked Stetson came around a bend in the marble stairs. The surprised Billy Vail called down, "What in thunder are you doing in Denver, Longarm? Seems I just got a wire from the Indian Nation saying

174

you'd missed Adeline Dalton by a hair and that she was bound for the Cherokee Strip.''

As Longarm joined them at the head of the stairs Vail added, ''Does this look like the Cherokee Strip, you poor, bewildered cuss?''

Longarm smiled thinly and said, ''I sent that wire night-letter rates to save money whilst I was still trying to make sense of unrelated facts I just couldn't fit together. By the time you could have been reading that night letter, Monday morning, I'd already blue-streaked up to Coffeyville to get rid of some ponies and pick up some express train tickets. Have they found Wee Willy guilty yet?''

Vail grumbled, ''They haven't even started in there. Took 'em two whole days just to pick a jury. Have you any notion how hard it can be to find twelve men good and true with no interest in a case that's been carried by every paper printed in English this side of the Big Muddy?''

As if to prove Vail's point, the federal prosecutor's pretty secretary came out to join them, blushed becomingly at the sight of Longarm, and asked Billy Vail, ''Have any of you seen Deputy Epworth from Moffat County? Mr. Clayburn wants to call him as the first prosecution witness and—''

''I thought he was inside with the rest of you,'' Billy Vail cut in, adding, ''I'm not even a lawyer, and I can see how your boss has no case without the witness Emma Ferguson gasped her last words at!''

Guilfoyle whistled thoughtfully and said, ''Epworth has been staying at the Colfax, and someone tried to get Longarm here, right after we brung Wee Willy in! Want me to scoot over there, boss?''

Vail shook his head and said, ''We'll give him a few more minutes. The gun slicks out to do our Longarm were more worried about covering up for Frank and Jesse than any two-bit kidnapper-killer.''

Longarm was just about to say they were both sniffing at the wrong trees when Flynn, down the corridor, whistled for their attention and they turned as one to see two other

Stetsons rising from the other stairwell. Vail said, "It's about time." and the perky, blue-eyed brunette who rode herd on Clayburn's legal briefs said, "Goody, with Deputy Epworth here we can start the trial!"

Longarm softly asked her which was the Moffat County deputy who'd come upon the dead and dying Fergusons. Maureen said Epworth was the younger one under the pearl-gray Stetson. Gals paid more attention to colors than things like tied-down Colt Lightnings. She said the older one with the bushy mustache was Epworth's boss, Undersheriff Drake.

As the Colorado lawmen approached, the older one spied Maureen tapping a dainty foot and called out, "Sleeping Beauty, here, ain't used to your heavier air down here. He'd still be slugabed if I hadn't banged on his fool door."

The nice-looking but sort of weak-jawed Epworth smiled sheepishly at the gal, locked eyes with Longarm, and went all ashy-faced. But nothing serious happened until Longarm called out, "Would you mind stepping clear of Deputy Epworth, sir?"

Undersheriff Drake never did. His younger deputy never gave him time to come unstuck before that Colt Lightning was out of its tie-down holster with lethal intent. He was even faster than Longarm had expected, but having expected it, Longarm naturally sat him flat on his ass with two rounds in the chest before he could hurt anyone. Then Longarm let the derringer he'd been palming drop to the end of its watch chain as he drew his more serious six-gun. But Undersheriff Drake had been too smart, or too frozen, to go for his own. Billy Vail was covering Drake, too, as he soberly said, "Guilfoyle, keep everyone inside that courtroom until I find out what this was all about. What was this all about, Longarm?"

Longarm moved in to disarm Drake and drop to one knee by the deputy he'd downed before he said, "This one's in no position now to tell us whether he was acting alone or in cahoots with this other gent. So let's just keep open minds

176

before we either charge him or hand his gun back to him.''

Drake protested, ''Charge me with what, you damned fools? Oops, sorry, ma'am.''

Maureen nodded at him and stamped her foot at Longarm as she said, ''Custis, you're being awfully silly this morning! The man we're trying for killing the Fergusons is inside with the judge and jury right now. So why did you just kill our star witness, you big goof?''

Before Longarm could answer, the oak door behind Maureen opened a mite despite Guilfoyle, and Prosecutor Clayburn spilled out into the hall along with Deputy Cohan. Guilfoyle enlisted Cohan, and together they got the door shut again while Clayburn did a sort of war dance over the body at their feet, even more upset about it than his secretary. Longarm said, ''I'm glad you were able to join us, pard. Mayhaps it'll learn you that justice should be blind but not downright stupid. Seeing as Epworth was stupid enough to tip his mitt by slapping leather before I'd even charged him, we ought to be able to tidy things up here, so's neither the *Post* nor the *News* can make any of us look too stupid.''

Billy Vail demanded, ''Longarm, will you cut out all this professional courtesy and just tell us why you shot that old boy there? I can see you had something on him. I agree his guilty conscience gave you a swell chance to prove his guilt. But what in thunder was he guilty of?''

''Oh, that's easy,'' said Longarm. ''It all fell in place for me the other night at the Pawnee Agency on the Arkansas, right after I'd purely eliminated anyone in or about the Indian Nation as a sensible suspect. Once it occurred to me that most of the serious killers I'd met up with since expressing some doubt about the Ferguson case hailed from around here, not around there, and once I'd been told by more than one poor, lonesome gal how dreary life can get on an Indian reserve—''

''I'll dreary you if you don't get to the point!'' roared Vail.

So Longarm holstered his six-gun and reeled in his derringer as he said, "It only works one way as soon as you assume somebody with Colorado connections and a small fortune at his disposal was sending hired guns after me. Wee Willy Wiggins had no sensible motive, even for a total fool. I never arrested him. I was the only lawman in the world who was willing to listen to his sad story."

Vail warned, "Damn it, Longarm," and even Clayburn said, "It's safe to assume that's not Willy Wiggins you just shot it out with. So you're saying Epworth just made up that story about Emma Ferguson accusing Wiggins with her dying breath?"

Longarm nodded and said, not unkindly, "I knew you had to be smarter than you looked. Wee Willy was in no way involved in the case, beyond his being a handy saddle bum with a record as a sex fiend."

He reached for a smoke as he continued, "Epworth, there, was sort of raping Emma Ferguson regular, *with her permission*. She being a plain but lusty old gal with a homely husband who likely bored her silly."

Maureen, who likely read those mushy books about lonesome gals stuck out on moors with boring husbands, gasped, "Then you're saying Emma Ferguson was never kidnapped in the first place! It's your notion she and this two-faced lawman simply ran off together!"

Longarm struck a light for his cheroot and got it going before he shook out the match, saying, "It wasn't all that simple. Having seen tintypes of the late Emma Ferguson, I suspect he was at least as interested in her husband's bankroll as he could have been in her fair, white body."

Prosecutor Clayburn snapped his fingers and exclaimed, "The ransom note demanded exactly what Hamish Ferguson had in his savings account! The false-hearted lover must have gotten that from the poor Indian agent's cheating wife!"

Longarm smiled fondly at him and said, "You see how easy it gets once you consider it's barely possible Wee Willy was telling the truth? That's how come the real killer got so excited once he heard even one lawman of my experience was paying a lick of attention to Wee Willy. He knew his own guilt or innocence rested in his own word, and his own word *alone*! He never presented a lick of evidence, save for simply *saying* he'd tagged along after Hamish Ferguson, heard shots, and arrived to discover the kidnapper had pulled a deadly double cross on all concerned.''

It was Undersheriff Drake who gasped first. ''I see it! And to think it was me the rascal first reported the crime to—another way than it happened, I mean. I could kick myself in the head for being such a dolt. It never occurred to me to doubt him.''

Vail growled, ''You should have, but welcome to the dolt club. Once you even consider a man lying about money, as often as that's been known to happen, you can see that Epworth never followed nobody nowhere. He was waiting, with his willing kidnap victim, when her poor simp of a husband rid in with the money to get her back.''

Maureen decided, ''She must have agreed with her lover on the final payoff. I mean, the way she thought it was *supposed* to turn out. He'd told her they'd just murder poor Hamish Ferguson and ride off with his life savings to live happily ever after in his rose-covered castle in the air, right?''

Longarm nodded grimly and said, ''Old Epworth, there, wasn't the rose-covered-castle type, and even if she'd looked more like Miss Cinderella or Snow White, she'd have still been a witness as could hang him, and even worse, he'd have had to share the money with her. So he gunned them both down good. We just saw how good he could be with that double-action six-gun.''

He took a thoughtful drag on his cheroot, choosing his next words carefully in mixed company before he said, ''The coroner's report would back his tale of the dead woman's complaints about indelicate abuse. She'd been camped out with him under, ah, unsanitary romantic conditions. He'd

179

already picked out Wee Willy to hang for his crimes. All he had to do was *say* the dead woman had accused the poor, unpopular ex-convict, track him down to the, ah, house of ill repute he was known to frequent, and—''

"Hold on," objected Undersheriff Drake. "Have you forgotten those odd hoof marks leading from the murder scene to that, ah, place you just mentioned?"

Longarm answered simply, "I never saw them. Did you?"

Drake started to nod, gasped instead, and said, "Suffering snakes! It's no wonder he was out to have you shot in the back to shut you up! His whole plan hinged on nobody paying a lick of attention to a dim-witted petty crook arrested on no more than his say-so!"

Over by the door, Deputy Cohan called out, "Hey, Marshal Vail? We got us a steamed up federal judge, here, threatening us with Leavenworth or worse if we don't let him out! Can he really hand out life at hard for contempt of court?"

Vail laughed and said, "We'd best not risk it. Just make sure nobody else gets out until we tidy up this hallway a mite."

As the judge bore down on them, flapping in his robes like an enraged crow, Vail called out, "It's not as bad as it looks, Your Honor."

But the judge said he'd be the judge of that, and with one thing and the other it was way into afternoon before Billy Vail was finally able to get alone in his own office down the hall with Longarm. Once he had, Vail kicked the door shut and rummaged in a file cabinet for a couple of hotel tumblers and a pint of rye, saying, "So much for all that bullshit about the Ferguson case. I still don't have your troubles in the Indian Nation straight in my head, old son. You say that tip about Jesse James visiting his distant kin, the Daltons, was stale news?"

Longarm reached for the heroic drink Billy poured him as he nodded and replied, "A Cheyenne breed from Colorado heard some half-ass rumors in Osage country. He was likely just considering the bounty on Frank and Jesse when he wrote his old pal, Epworth, about that horse-trading Mister Howard. Epworth would have long since read the same Pinkerton reports on the Daltons as the rest of us got. Like myself, he'd no doubt dismissed Adeline Dalton as too wild a shot to consider, next to the Millers, the Fords, and other such folk a heap closer to the clan's old Missouri stomping grounds. But once he'd failed to have me taken out here in Denver, he decided I'd die way more convenient for him out of this state entire.''

Vail nodded and said, ''Then it was *him* as engineered that swell tip to lure you off to the Indian Nation.''

Longarm started to say it had never been his own notion to go. He sipped some rye instead, and said, ''Good stuff. I doubt we'll ever know how many owl-hoot riders with Colorado connections were sent after me or just hiding out there to begin with. From the piss-poor job they did for a crooked lawman they all knew and admired, I doubt he could have offered much for killing me, and to tell the truth, I feel just a mite insulted about that.''

Billy said soothingly, ''Hell, they've only posted five hundred on Billy the Kid so far, and he's even more famous than you.''

Billy finished his drink and poured himself another as he went on. ''I follows your drift about your drifting through the Indian Nation meeting up with pals of Deputy Epworth, Jesse James, and so forth. I'm still a might fuzzy on just how our Dingus and Buck fit into your final report.''

Longarm assured him, ''Henry will have enough to type up in triplicate if I leave the dumb stuff out. It may be worth noting that either of the James boys could be using Howard or even Woodson, as well as Miller, Ford, or Chadwell. I felt no call to doubt Frank Dalton's assurance that neither James has been in close contact with Cole Younger's poor old Aunt Adeline. We drew a blank on Frank and Jesse that time you sent me to pester Belle Starr, too, as I recall.''

Vail nodded grudgingly but insisted, "You still come closer this time. Sooner or later we're going to catch them boys, hiding out with distant kith or kin. Everyone's watching their *close* kith and kin."

Longarm shrugged and said, "It's still likely they'll be caught for us by members of their widespread clan. It's spread out way too thin and commencing to show wear spots, Billy. Younger members like the Dalton brothers don't remember riding against the damn Yankees for the Lost Cause. Since President Hayes got rid of the last dumb Reconstruction laws, it just looks like bank robbing or stopping trains to kids like the ones I just met, and young Frank has applied for a federal badge like you and I pack."

Vail sighed and said, "I'll bet you kids related to Cole Younger turn out no better, with or without his excuses. But I can see why you decided to come on home, and all things considered, I'm glad you did. Hanging the wrong man could have given more ammunition to them assholes who want to do away with the death penalty back East."

Longarm looked wistfully at the window behind Vail's desk as he replied, "Well, mayhaps I'll just drift over to the Parthenon and compose my thoughts before I put it all down on paper for you in the morning."

Vail said, "Wrong. I'll refill your glass and I'll even let you sip it out front where visitors might see you doing it. But if you think you're knocking off a full damned hour before quitting time with at least a ten-page report for Henry to type up, you are sadly mistook, and mayhaps I'd best not let you drink any more until you talk more sensible!"

Longarm said he felt sensible enough, damn it. So Vail refilled his glass and let him go out to pester Henry for a legal pad and a pencil with an eraser on it this time, for chrissakes.

Then he sat at a corner writing table the priss said he could use and used it until it was quitting time and change. As Henry rose from his own desk, rolling down the sleeve garters he used to keep his fool cuffs out of the inkwell, he asked how Longarm was coming with that report.

Longarm growled, "I'm not about to quit this close to the end. I just figured out how to report my conversation with Frank and Grat Dalton without dragging a lady's name through it needless. You go on along, Henry. I'll not only lock up, but, hell, I'll even leave all this paper on your desk for you."

Henry said he wished Longarm wouldn't. He said to just leave the report where it was, if he ever finished it, and then the priss put his coat and straw skimmer on to leave Longarm laboring on as the rest of Denver headed home for supper.

He'd missed his free lunch at the Parthenon, come to study on it. So as he scribbled on, his stomach growling, he cussed the heart and soul of the asshole who'd first put down that bull about virtue being its own reward. He was tempted to pack it in for the night before he ate the damned pencil like a damned beaver. But he'd been telling the truth when he'd told Henry he was getting there. So he just kept going until he got there, then blinked and muttered, "Son of a bitch, I've *finished* this fool literary effort all of a sudden!"

Then there was nothing to do but sign his name, get stiffly to his feet, pull his hat brim more Cavalry as he strode to the front door, making sure the spring latch was set, and simply leave. For if Billy Vail was still somewhere in the back, it was between Billy and his old woman, holding supper on him up to Sherman Avenue.

Thinking about supper in connection with Sherman Avenue reminded Longarm of a certain fashionable young widow woman who lived up that way as well. She'd no doubt be pleased to learn he was back in town, alive, after all his lonely nights in Indian country. He never asked her how she spent her lonely nights in Denver when he was out in the field, either. That was likely one of the reasons they were such good pals.

But as he stepped out into the now mighty gloomy cor-

183

ridor, a bright, chipper voice called out, "Oh, Custis! I was so afraid you'd already left for the day!"

As he smiled down at the pretty little blue-eyed brunette from Clayburn's office, he said, "I can't leave for the day, now, Miss Maureen. It's already evening."

She laughed and burbled, "Don't I ever know it. I've been taking shorthand till my poor little fingers need someone to kiss 'em and make 'em well. We've decided Deputy Epworth was working alone, or at least that he has no surviving confederates, thanks to you. So we just turned Willy Wiggins loose, and you owe Undersheriff Drake an apology the next time you meet up with him."

He hesitated, then he said he'd rather kiss her fingers than tell anyone he was sorry. So she asked if they could grab just a bite of real food first, and he said he surely admired a gal who shared *all* his carnal appetites, adding, "I was just cussing the old fool who said virtue was its own reward. Now I don't find him half as foolish. For had I shirked my duty whilst you were doing your own, there's no telling who either one of us would have wound up eating with this evening, honey."

She dimpled up at him, took the elbow he offered, and showed she was a good old gal, too, by observing, "I'm sure you'd have found someone. But I'm sort of glad it was me."

And so they proved that virtue was indeed its own reward, because the next time he called on that widow woman on Sherman Avenue, she believed he'd just gotten back to town, and it never would have worked the other way, of course.

184

Watch for

LONGARM AND THE LOST MINE

142nd novel in the bold LONGARM series
from Jove

Coming in October!

A special offer for people who enjoy reading the best Westerns published today. If you enjoyed this book, subscribe now and get . . .

TWO FREE

A $5.90 VALUE—NO OBLIGATION

If you enjoyed this book and would like to read more of the very best Westerns being published today, you'll want to subscribe to True Value's Western Home Subscription Service. If you enjoyed the book you just read and want more of the most exciting, adventurous, action packed Westerns, subscribe now.

Each month the editors of True Value will select the 6 very best Westerns from America's leading publishers for special readers like you. You'll be able to preview these new titles as soon as they are published, FREE for ten days with no obligation.

TWO FREE BOOKS

When you subscribe, we'll send you your first month's shipment of the newest and best 6 Westerns for you to preview. With your first shipment, two of these books will be yours as our introductory gift to you absolutely FREE, regardless of what you decide to do. If you like them, as much as we think you will, keep all six books but pay for just 4 at the low subscriber rate of just $2.45 each. If you decide to return them, keep 2 of the titles as our gift. No obligation.

Special Subscriber Savings

When you become a True Value subscriber you'll save money several ways. First, all regular monthly selections will be billed at the low subscriber price of just $2.45 each. That's

WESTERNS!

at least a savings of $3.00 each month below the publishers price. Second, there is never any shipping, handling or other hidden charges—Free home delivery. What's more there is no minimum number of books you must buy, you may return any selection for full credit and you can cancel your subscription at any time. A TRUE VALUE!

Mail the coupon below

To start your subscription and receive 2 FREE WESTERNS, fill out the coupon below and mail it today. We'll send your first shipment which includes 2 FREE BOOKS as soon as we receive it.

4-11-07

Explore the exciting Old West with
one of the men who made it wild!